Staged

A CUPID/PSYCHE FAKE DATING NOVELLA

REBECCA V. ARCHER

GOLDEN ALE PRESS LLC

Ebook ISBN 979-8-9885247-0-0

Paperback ISBN 979-8-9885247-1-7

Edited by Arielle Haughee of Orange Blossom Publishing

Proofread by Laura Helseth of Read Head Editing

Cover Designed by Wolfsparrow Publishing

Interior Art by Taryn Siegle

For Wesley

Contents

Author's Note/Content Warning

This book is a Cupid and Psyche retelling. In the original myth, Psyche does not know Cupid's identity. This part of the myth is retained. However, the sex between Will and Alma is consensual.

Other content warnings include auto accidents, references to misogyny experienced by characters, references to sexual harassment, emotional manipulation by parents (off page for children, on page for adults). This list may not be inclusive. Please see the author's website for any updates or additions.

www.rebeccavarcher.com/staged

Chapter One

ALMA BLAKE STARED AT THE MAN BEFORE HER IN confusion. First, he wore a mask in the middle of the afternoon while wearing a tailored suit. The mask was a simple domino, and he looked like a cross between a rich playboy and a superhero.

She bit the inside of her lip to keep from laughing.

Second, she didn't understand the job.

"I'm an actor, not an escort," she said.

"I understand. I'm paying you to pretend to be my girlfriend. Not to be my girlfriend," he said. He'd introduced himself as Will, but provided no other information. The mask was a good indication he cared about privacy above all else.

"I still think an escort is more qualified even if you don't use all her services," Alma said.

The man chuckled. "Would you be insulted if I said you are more economical than an escort?"

"I should adjust my rates." She spoke out of her ass. This was not a normal job where she knew how much to charge. She mostly worked in theater productions. Denver had a great performing arts center, and she'd gotten a lot of fantastic roles.

True, after her last show ended, she hadn't found a new play. On top of that, her day job suffocated her. This was a chance for her to earn some money and branch out. Maybe take a chance in a new city.

And really, any acting was better than the administrative work she did at her father's law firm.

"The job is simple. Eros opens this Thursday. I need someone to help me host. For three nights, you dress up, drink expensive alcohol, and occasionally look at me like my presence is vital to your existence."

"Explain the masks, please," she said.

The sign on the building had a masquerade mask, and the advance research she did indicated the nightclub's dress code required all guests wear some sort of mask around their eyes. The exact design and details were left up to the patrons.

Will leaned forward on his desk, clasping his hands together. "Eros is an alternate universe from the rest of the clubs in the area. Here, you can be whoever you want without fear of judgment."

She wondered what he was hiding from.

She saw the appeal in masking. Too many people recognized her. She couldn't go out to bars or clubs without someone recognizing her and repeating lines to her from a commercial she did when she was six, then asking her to help them get a job.

Her father was one of the most influential people in the city. He owned the biggest law firm and was running for mayor. Her circumstances were unique. Anonymity might be freedom for her, but for someone else, it was more likely an excuse for crappy behavior.

"What if who you are is an asshole who wants to take advantage of other people?" she asked.

"We have strict limits on the amount of alcohol each

person is served. We designed the floor of the club so security is always close by. All our staff are trained in intervention."

"And it's not a sex thing?"

His cheeks turned a little pink. "It's not a sex thing."

She still had a thousand questions, but he appeared patient with her. "If I'm supposed to be your girlfriend, then is it an ongoing role? Or will you only need me for this weekend?" She didn't intend to commit herself to something longer.

"It's only opening weekend when I want someone by my side. After, if anyone asks, I'll say you're tucked in bed waiting for me, or we broke up. It won't matter. I won't need you. Your obligations and our relationship end on Sunday."

The way he said he wouldn't need her twisted her stomach. She was used to people climbing over themselves to get to her. It wasn't something she liked. But there was something about this man that made her wish their relationship wasn't just a transaction.

She didn't say anything, so he added. "I'll double what I already offered."

Alma chewed on the inside of her lip some more. She didn't know the rates for sex workers, but the numbers weren't economical anymore. This was a fair amount of money, enough to supplement her savings.

It wouldn't change her life, but it might move up her timeline.

"This will require improvisation. That's not my specialty."

"But you can do it?"

"Yes, but I don't want to set either one of us up for failure." Normally, she'd insist she could do whatever the job required, and then fake it. But this wasn't the usual job, and Alma wasn't sure it was worth fighting for.

"Can you fake desire?" Will, no last name, asked.

"If that's a question about my sex life, then it is highly

inappropriate." She grew up around lawyers, spent her non-acting days around lawyers. She could spot a successful lawsuit a mile away.

He smiled. Actually smiled, which was not something Alma thought he was capable of. Max, the woman who had walked her to his office, warned her Will could be severe.

"No, on stage. You've pretended to be attracted to someone you aren't and sell it to an audience, correct?"

"Well yes, but it takes work. We do chemistry reads at casting and then months of rehearsals so when the time comes, we trust each other."

"You don't trust me." He knew that wasn't a question.

"Of course not. We just met, and you won't show me your face."

He pondered her for a moment, then stood up and walked to her side of the desk. He offered her his hand as if to help her stand.

She accepted out of curiosity.

"Let's see if we have any chemistry then."

She stood in front of him, their feet almost touching. She tilted her face up to see into his blue eyes. Even with the mask, he was attractive. He peered into her eyes, and suddenly she wanted to be the one wearing a mask. She felt naked in front of him and needed something to protect her, or else he'd find out all her secrets and desires.

She turned away in self-preservation. "Uh, requiring me to kiss you on a job interview is definitely sexual harassment."

He flinched and stepped back, releasing her hand. "Don't worry. Any physical intimacies between us will be discussed in advance. Limits will be set with your comfort in mind and above mine. And before you ask, there is no scenario in which you will be required to have sex or remove your clothes in front of anyone. You have my absolute word."

That made her feel better. He clearly wanted to

communicate with her even if he completely sidestepped her statement on trust.

He could keep his secrets, that was fine with her. It was a job. She didn't need anything more from him.

"How do you intend to see if we have chemistry?" she asked. "Normally we read from the script."

"Okay." He stared at her intently as if he was trying to memorize her. "Pretend you are my girlfriend, and you've surprised me in my office."

Alma glanced around the room and willed herself into character. What kind of woman would this man date? The space was sparsely appointed with a sleek, black desk, walls with framed photographs of the Denver skyline, and a stiff leather couch. She thought about the club itself. It was a place where, if it lived up to its expectations, people could be wild and free.

Someone elegant and adventurous then. Someone who was the life of the party. That was what he was asking from her.

She was none of those things, but she could fake it.

"If I surprised you at work, you'd take your mask off."

"If that's a deal breaker for you, then let me know now. You won't see my face. Ever."

His eyes narrowed behind the mask. Somehow it wasn't a deal breaker. The money was good. She would see this through. But it felt like he was pushing her to back down, and that wasn't something she wanted to do.

Curiosity may kill the cat, but she'd take precautions. All their interactions would either be public or at his apartment. She'd give his address to her parents and if anything happened to her, they'd know where to find her. He was going out of his way to assure her of her safety.

"No, it's not a deal breaker."

He looked relieved and angry simultaneously.

She grabbed his hand and guided him to the couch. They sat, her angling toward him, getting as comfortable as possible in her tight dress.

Will tracked the hem as it moved up her thigh.

She was pretty; she knew that. It helped in her field. But knowing this man might find her attractive did things to her stomach. Even if he did wear a silly mask.

She held onto his hand. Her touch wouldn't go beyond this, not when they hadn't talked about intimacy. But he offered his first, so it was fair game.

She liked how his fingers felt against hers.

"Let's go away for a little bit," she said. "I know things are intense with the club opening, but it'll settle soon. I found a resort a few hours from here, and they have great weekday deals."

It was his turn to be confused so she tilted her head, indicating he should respond with something. They were acting like a couple...the exact thing they were supposed to do this weekend. If they couldn't communicate non-verbally, they were already set up to flop.

With his fingertips, he adjusted her hand so her palm faced up, sending shivers up her arm.

He noticed her reaction.

"Yeah? What is there to do at this resort?" His mouth turned up at one corner.

"There is a hot spring and a great restaurant." It was winter and the hot spring would be cozy. "It's not ski country, but they have snowmobiling and things like that." She imagined the resort in her head. She didn't have a specific place in mind, but she dreamt one up. She pictured string lights over steaming water, and her back against Will's chest as he played with the ties of her bikini.

Her cheeks flushed. She didn't need that image in her head while she was trying to be a professional.

He kept his attention on her hand. "You know, if we go somewhere, I'll be focused on keeping you in the room."

He wasn't helping her temperature problem. "We can do that here."

"So, you agree we don't need to leave?"

"Here's crowded," she said. "You live across the street from work. If we stay, you'll be distracted."

He gazed into her eyes, and his mask seemed to fade. "You give me this weekend, and I promise I'll give you two days of my undivided attention wherever you desire them."

His hand drifted to her wrist, her pulse racing against his fingertips.

This needed to stop before she lost herself in the fantasy.

"Deal," she said.

"Great." He released her, and her body jolted without his touch. She plastered a neutral expression across her face, watching as he retreated to his desk and handed her a notebook he pulled from a drawer. "Write down your measurements. I'll be providing your wardrobe. And you'll have to show up at the salon down the street early for hair and makeup."

She wrote down the numbers she had memorized. "Do I get a say on wardrobe?" She'd recently played Titania in Shakespeare's *A Midsummer Night's Dream*. The male director had insisted on very small costumes. She didn't want a repeat of that experience.

"It'll be to my taste. Simple."

"What if someone recognizes me?" she asked. This last question felt like preservation, a chance for her to escape rather than get close to him again.

"I doubt any of my patrons will be frequent attendees of the theater. Plus, you'll be wearing a mask, remember?"

That was oddly dismissive of his patrons, but she'd have to trust the mask. And him.

Incidentally, she had never been recognized for her theater work.

It crossed her mind to mention her father. Will had to know the connection. Any basic search of her showed it. But she kept silent. This job was about her and her skills alone. If Will didn't know about Charles Blake, that was his fault.

She'd relish in the rare occurrence someone wanted her for her and not that she brought them closer to her father.

After she placed the notebook down, Will dismissed her. "I have your number and email. I'll be in touch."

Alma stood up. "Great. I'll see you in a few days." She forced her face into a smile. She knew this was a job, and they were both acting, but she'd experienced more sparks with him in thirty seconds than she did with any boyfriend or date in the past. His abrupt behavior change hurt more than she expected it to.

He smiled. "I'm looking forward to it, Alma."

Will Caron tossed his mask aside as soon as Alma left, feeling conflicted and disgusted with himself. He tried to walk a line between making her an offer she couldn't refuse and insulting her to the point that she ran in the opposite direction.

He thought he'd almost succeeded in making her run.

Getting in her personal space was supposed to drive her away. He wouldn't subject her to sexual harassment, but he came as close as possible without stepping over the line.

All while assuring her he respected her boundaries.

It drew her closer to him, and he liked it. When they stood in front of each other, he'd almost kissed her—and she'd noticed. He'd never wanted another woman more than he wanted Alma. When she described their fake vacation, he'd been imagining those days with her. He wished she thought the same things. But any flush he saw from her was acting. The increase in her heartbeat was nerves. It had nothing to do with desire for him.

She didn't deserve what he was about to put her through.

His phone vibrated and he answered the call, already annoyed with the conversation.

"Did she agree?" his mother, Judy, asked.

"She did." He held his face in one hand and the phone in the other. He was lying to Alma, and he'd lie to his mother, but he only felt bad about one of them. "This will be harder than you think. She's smart. She won't be manipulated easily."

Judy tsked. "You can do it. Get her drunk and get her to take her clothes off in public, or get her drunk and seduce her and videotape it. I don't care what you do, just get some scandalous photos so we can ruin her father."

She sounded like a cartoon villain. She'd never been the best parent—everything had to be done her way. But he'd never doubted she cared. She just did it *her* way and left no room for disagreement.

That translated over to her career.

On paper, she was someone people looked up to. As Denver's first female mayor, she governed with compassion and put forward initiatives to help working families. She championed woman's rights and worked to make Denver a welcoming city for everyone. Will thought these things mattered to her; they probably did, once. But now her sole focus was staying in power.

In her crosshairs was Charles Blake—famous citywide for the cheesy commercials and billboards he ran for his law firm featuring his family as they grew up—and her opponent in the upcoming election. They had similar beliefs and political philosophies and had been friends years ago. Both were powerful people, but in their separate silos. Once Charles encroached on Judy's, her defenses went up and she started to throw punches.

Covertly, of course. She'd never do anything in public to weaken her image.

But she would stage a scenario in which Charles Blake's youngest daughter was caught behaving badly.

Lucky for Judy, she had a son the same age as Alma, and he had a brand-new nightclub to provide cover for her scheme.

"It's not too late to turn around your campaign, get more volunteers, hire better consultants."

"Don't get cold feet on me. If you don't cooperate, I will cut your funding."

He clenched his teeth. When he accepted her loan to open Eros, the terms were generous. Not many investors or banks saw a young man opening a nightclub where everyone was required to hide their identity as a good investment. His mother stepped in when no one else did. He'd expected the money would eventually come with extra strings, but he didn't expect she'd fuck with him this early.

It was so like her to give him something, and as soon as he showed he cared, rip it from him.

As a child, every toy she gave him came with the condition that he keep his room clean to her standards. If he didn't, the toy would go right into the trash. It was easier to fall in line. Maybe it was time he stopped going along with her every whim.

"I'll do what I can." That was the lie he gave her. He wouldn't hurt Alma. He'd take her to Eros, but he'd ensure no one took advantage and that she made it home safely at the end of each night.

It was three days. He'd protect her. Even from himself.

"Good. I expect frequent updates."

She ended the call.

He pulled the program out of his drawer for *A Midsummer Night's Dream*. He'd gone in the name of research, to see his target in action.

She'd completely blown him out of the water with her talent. It was her show, and everyone else was there to support her. He never intended to go along with his mother's plan. But after seeing her perform, it was more than that.

He'd hung out after the show, debating if he should approach her. He wanted to ask her out. It wouldn't have been random. They went to middle school together. Their parents had been friends, once upon a time. It would have been normal for him to introduce himself and ask her to get a drink. They could have talked about what it was like to be a "first kid" of Denver. He was possibly the one person who understood what it was like to be the child of someone constantly in the spotlight like that.

But he couldn't lose his club, so he watched her sign autographs and then slip backstage, ending his chance to do something other than what he was supposed to. He'd go through the motions with Alma and pretend he was doing everything his mother asked, even if it wasn't his intention.

A knock on his door jolted him to the present.

"Hey, boss. It's me." It was the voice of his head server, Max. He instructed her to come in, not bothering to replace the mask on his face. Of his staff, she alone knew who he was and had seen his face.

"She get out okay?" he asked when she closed the door behind her.

"Yes, I'm wondering... What's happening?"

Once Eros opened, she would oversee all his VIP guests, including Alma.

"She's to act as my girlfriend this weekend and help me with hosting duties."

"Why?"

"She's charming." He didn't say Alma would be there for him. But that was a part of it. If he had a girlfriend, he'd want her there. Someone for him to turn to and watch with him as the world he created opened. This weekend was about his patrons, but he selfishly wanted one person to be there just for him.

"Are you sure about her? I recognize her from those Blake Smith ads. Isn't everyone in that family a lawyer?"

Music to his mother's ears.

"Alma is an actor. She's done a lot of work at the performing arts center. And she won't be recognizable. She'll be wearing makeup, and it will be dark. No one will notice."

"Right. I hope she helps you however you need her. If she agreed, you must have been pleasant to her, and I'll tolerate any change that makes you a nicer person."

"I'm not mean," he protested. They'd worked together closely for years, ever since he got his first bartending job and she carried his drinks. Max earned the right to give him a hard time.

"You're not anything, Will. You basically have no personality. You used to, but then you let this place consume you. If she brings out your personality, then I am all for it."

"Right, well can you keep this between us and work with the salon down the street on some looks for her?"

"Sure thing." She winked and then left.

Will sank into his seat. If he could do this, he'd get a few days with an amazing woman and be able to keep his club without pissing off his mother. If there was a balance to be struck, he'd find it.

Chapter Two

On Thursday, Alma's closet was strewn across her bedroom. Her father, Charles, stood in the door frame.

"Walk me through this again." His movie-star looks served him well as Denver's best trial lawyer. His smile graced countless billboards and TV ads. Witnesses crumbled under his glare.

Alma had grown accustomed, but it still irritated her when he used it on her.

"It's opening weekend of a new club. The owner wants me to pose as his girlfriend and share some of the hosting duties." She folded a pair of leggings. Will was providing the clothes she needed for the club, so she only needed to pack loungewear and pajamas.

"He should hire an actual employee. One with event planning experience. Why are you staying at his place?" His tone was obvious to her, even if it wasn't to someone else. He might not say it out loud, but what he really cared about was Alma not spending her entire weekend volunteering for his campaign.

"He lives across from the club. It'll be an easy commute, and it's more believable."

"I don't like this." The fact that Charles took time out of his day to discuss this with her showed how much he didn't like it. His time was valuable. He told her this repeatedly growing up.

She was the youngest of his three daughters, and he spent much of their childhood working to grow his legal practice. He wasn't around much, leaving most of the parenting to their mother. If he did get involved, it meant she was in trouble.

Alma was twenty-six now, but the same dynamics applied.

"Dad, it's fine. I signed the contract. I'm doing this."

He pinched the bridge of his nose. "Tell me you didn't sign a legal document without me reviewing it."

"I read it thoroughly. It's three days, and if he does anything to make me uncomfortable, I'll leave."

"Let me see it." She pulled up the PDF on her phone and handed the device to him. He spent the next few minutes immersed, so Alma used this distraction to pack her underwear and bras. "It's a non-disclosure written more in your favor than I would if I was him."

"I have learned a thing or two working for the firm."

"You need to be careful. After that blog came out, your life is fair game for commentary," Charles said, setting her phone down.

That was another reason Alma looked forward to getting away and being someone else. A few days earlier, a conservative blog had a post about how her theater costumes corrupted Denver's youth. It was sexist and slut-shaming and, instead of letting it go unnoticed, the media picked up the story to come to her defense. No one asked if she wanted the attention. They talked about choices made for her by the men in her life without giving her the chance to add her voice.

No one talked about how much work she put into her performance, or the rave reviews the show's entire run got. Only about how her appearance affected men.

She texted Will to ask if he wanted to reconsider hiring her. He didn't address the article and instead sent her pictures of the dresses he selected for her approval. He was right; they were simple. Short with solid colors. Not what she normally wore. The necklines were a little lower than she was used to, but well within reason. She'd be stylish and fit in with the patrons of the club, but she wouldn't appear on any blog site for them.

"I'm always well-behaved. And I'm working."

"Perception matters more than reality."

She wondered if he was more concerned about something bad happening to her or if her existence was a distraction.

He crossed his arms. "Your last play is done. You haven't booked any auditions. The application deadline for Colorado Law closes in two weeks."

She clenched her jaw. "I didn't agree to that."

"You can go to law school and still act in small productions."

"That's your goal for me. It's never been mine."

"What is your plan then?"

She didn't want to tell him the truth about what she was working toward. She intended for things to be in motion before she brought it up. "I'm fine with how things are. I appreciate my job at the firm. I'm doing well with acting. *Midsummer* got great reviews. I'll get another job. It takes time; you know that."

"You get preferential treatment at the firm. You're taking time off when you haven't accrued it."

"I'm a part-time employee. I work the hours I'm required."

"We need you full-time."

Alma froze. "What do you mean?"

"Your role at the firm is changing. You can either be a full-time employee, or we'll have to let you go."

"Why? What's happened?" There hadn't been any conversation about her hours changing. The firm had plenty of part-time employees—parents who needed the flexibility for childcare, college students exploring law for the first time. Hell, at least two people she knew worked part-time while they pursued side hustles they hoped to make full-time.

"A few of the other admins have complained about your preferential treatment. And there is more than enough work to go around. Your sisters live up to the same expectations as every other associate. So should you."

Her sisters constantly did what he asked. Both went to law school right after undergrad and then worked their asses off to get maximum billable hours every year.

They were quintessential, model lawyers.

"But I'm not an associate. My role is different. This is sudden. I thought you were happy about my limited hours since I can volunteer for your campaign." As she talked, she realized this was an excuse to manipulate her into doing what he wanted her to do. He'd force her to make a choice. "Why is this so important to you?"

"I built Blake Smith from the ground up. It provided me with the stability to have a family and the life I want. You're an amazing actress. But you've been working the theater scene for four years. It hasn't paid off. It's time to try something new."

"Acting is my passion. Not law. I can find another job. Somewhere not Blake Smith."

He nodded. "I'm sure. You're incredibly smart and talented. You understand when I become mayor, I can't show favoritism to anyone, including my family. Oh, and we will discuss you paying rent when you return."

He closed the door behind him when he left, leaving Alma

at a loss for words. He'd supported her career in acting and boasted to everyone who listened about what role she had been cast in. She was aware his patience wore thin, but this was a level of malice she hadn't expected. Not once in her life had he ever set his mind to something and not gotten it. He thought he had her right where he wanted her, so dependent on him she'd cave and follow his plan for her. He didn't believe she'd survive without him. Alma already intended to break out from the family sphere. This weekend with Will would help her get closer to that goal. She'd figure out what to do with her dad and her day job when this was over.

She wouldn't give up her dream so she'd fit into some idyllic version of the family business her father wanted.

LATER THAT DAY, ALMA FIDGETED WITH THE KEY IN her hand, remembering the smile Will gave her.

She'd stopped by prior to the salon to drop off her bag, and he gave her a quick tour of the apartment. He wore his mask, of course, and though his guard was up, he seemed genuinely happy to see her.

She expected dark colors and the casually thrown togetherness she associated with the apartments of single men in their twenties. She got simple navy-blue furniture with hard lines. Like the couch in his office, it was for appearances rather than comfort. Everything looked brand new, like it belonged in the pages of a catalog. If she expected to get any hint of who he was from his living space, she was mistaken.

He handed her a key and told her to make herself at home. She needed to run down the street to get her hair and makeup done, but he promised to go over boundaries and expectations later.

The salon was busier than Alma anticipated. Her stylist

described how Eros opening provided them with new opportunities. They advertised extending their hours for people to come in beforehand and get a proper look. They filled their Instagram with experiments from the previous weeks, and their appointments were fully booked for the evening.

Alma beamed with pride at the thought her boyfriend was responsible for creating a new subculture in the city and supporting others.

Fake boyfriend, she reminded herself.

She had spent the days since her interview trying to dig up information on Club Eros and its owner but came up with little. He did a few advance interviews, but they had been vague on details about who he was as a person.

One article featured pictures of him in an artful shadow.

It was sexy to look at.

She turned the key in the lock and held her breath, afraid for a moment of Will's reaction to seeing her. The salon had specific instructions from him on how to do her hair and makeup.

The makeup was far out of her comfort zone. She hadn't worn anything like it without being on stage. It was done in the style of a masquerade mask. The artist drew an intricate pattern of gold lines around her eyes and across the bridge of her nose. It looked like she stepped out of a fairy tale. She wouldn't have to wear a physical mask to hide her identity; it was all done with makeup.

She walked into the kitchen, and Will turned to face her.

They both froze.

He wore a gold mask, framing his eyes with fine lines etched across it in the same pattern as her mask. They were a matching set.

"Perfect," he said. "You look perfect."

She didn't realize how much she needed to hear that. In

addition to the makeup, she asked the stylist if they had time to change her hair color. After the week with her being the center of attention, she wanted to be someone different.

In addition to the blowout and subtle waves, the stylist darkened her hair from blonde to medium brown.

"I should have asked about the hair first," she said. "I'll pay you for it. They said you have an account, and it was covered, but this is outside of what you asked for."

"No, it's beautiful. You look stunning," he said. "The color is great. It suits you."

Her cheeks warmed at the praise.

"I'm impressed the makeup is so pretty without it looking like face paint," Alma said.

"She's the best around, and I won't have anything less for my girlfriend."

"No, I guess not."

Will gestured to the table. "Have a seat. You need to eat before we go." He pulled a plate out of the oven and set it down in front of her. "Chicken with Mexican rice and assorted vegetables."

She dug into the roasted carrots as he poured her a glass of wine. "I shouldn't. I don't drink very much, and I'm a bit of a lightweight."

"One with me now and one with me when we get to the club. After, we'll both switch to non-alcoholic drinks." He sat down at the table with her. He appeared remarkably calm, considering tonight was the cumulation of over a year's worth of work for him and years of dreaming. The window from his living room looked down at the street, and while it was still an hour from opening, people were forming a line at the door of Club Eros.

"Okay." His confidence in her was magnetic. She desperately wanted to live up to his expectations. But as she got into character as his girlfriend, she needed to adjust her perspective. She was there for hosting responsibilities, but also, she was there for him. To support him, however he needed her.

"How's the dinner?" he asked, breaking her out of her thoughts. She couldn't place the tone in his voice.

"It's great, thank you." Then realization struck her. "You made it?"

"I did. Nightclubs aren't the only thing I can do." He shifted like he was trying to hide his happiness at her liking his cooking. She was skeptical he sought her approval. He lived in a beautiful apartment and owned a stunning nightclub. He had everything. Why did he need some employee to care about his cooking skills?

"Well, I'm impressed." If he thought she was blown away by him, maybe he would be blown away by her. And she *was* impressed. She even burned pasta once.

"We should talk about ground rules," he said, standing up and leaning against the counter. "How much touching are you comfortable with?"

She had thought about this in advance. They needed to pretend to be two people who slept together and were relaxed around each other. She wished they had spent more time rehearsing together. "I think I'm comfortable with a lot. Just keep your hands away from my...bikini areas." She blushed, needing to be explicit with him, but also imagining what his hands would feel like if there weren't rules. "We can get the message across without any public groping."

He nodded. "What about kissing?"

"I guess for that, follow my lead. You said you are more concerned with my comfort than your own. If you let me take the lead, then I'll stop anything before it gets too far."

"You'll tell me? I have no interest in pushing you into a corner and making you do something you don't want to do." His face showed concern. It was obvious to her that he completely understood she was the vulnerable one and didn't wish to take advantage of her.

"I will. Do we need a safe word or something?"

That earned her a laugh. "No, tell me to stop, and I'll stop. It'll be loud, so I doubt anyone will overhear us. But your comfort is more important than anything else. If we have to break character, then we will."

Her confidence in the situation grew. He'd deferred to her on so many things already. She was sure he wouldn't intentionally overstep. And if she stayed sober as she intended, then she'd be able to leave if things didn't turn out as she expected.

"And it's not like we'll need to make out in public or anything. We need to demonstrate affection for each other, not engage in foreplay," she said.

Will turned from her to put the wine in the fridge. "I can handle that."

WHILE WILL FINISHED UP THE DISHES, ALMA retreated to the bedroom to change. He was going to spend the next three nights on the couch. He didn't love the idea of sleeping so close to her and not being able to be with her, but he'd do anything to keep her comfortable.

He'd maintain his distance from Alma when they were in his apartment. She was already under his skin. He wanted to unpack her bag for her and see her toiletries lined up on the sink next to his. He wanted her to invade his space and make it her own.

Make it theirs.

The apartment was barely his space anyway. He moved in to be close to the club on the nights he worked. He rented another apartment a few miles from downtown that he considered his home. But he liked the idea of sharing this with her. It was fresh and ready to be filled with her scent and her voice.

He wondered what she slept in.

He loved what she'd done with her hair. It provided her an extra layer of protection. His mother would hate it, but he wasn't on his mother's side this weekend.

He heard her voice behind him. "Hey, can you zip me?"

"Sure." Her back was toward him, and the expanse of exposed skin made his mouth run dry. *She's my employee,* he reminded himself. He needed to stay professional.

He carefully raised the zipper and avoided touching her as much as possible.

"How does it fit?"

He didn't need her to respond. The green fabric clung to her curves. It accentuated her ass then finished in a light ruffle.

"It's great." She turned around, and his eyes immediately went to the straight neckline.

"I can see you're already practicing being amazed by me." She crossed the room and sat down on the couch to put on her shoes.

She hadn't been this confident before. Getting into costume must help her get into character. He liked the confidence.

He liked her before, too.

Will finished his wine. "You ready?" She captivated him as she bent to reach her feet. The shoes enhanced the muscles of her calves.

She stood and moved so she was toe to toe with him. Even in her heels, she was still several inches shorter. She looked at him, her mouth close enough that only the tiniest movement would be needed to claim her lips. He loved the way the makeup highlighted her eyes with the same markings as his mask.

Everyone would know she was his.

"Ready."

A half smirk passed her lips for the briefest second, and he remembered what was happening.

He was paying her to act. She wasn't interested in him, and if she found out the reason she was hired, she would be angry at being used.

This was all an act. One she was proud of.

Chapter Three

WILL THOUGHT WALKING INTO HIS CLUB ON opening night would be a different experience than it was. He thought he'd absorb everything around him—the people dancing, getting drinks, and enjoying the world he created.

But instead, he focused on the woman next to him. The motion of her body through the crowd, the bounce of her hair, and the feeling of her fingers intertwined with his.

Will steered her to the VIP section. Since it was early, only a handful of people occupied the space. He introduced Alma to the bouncer, Ben, who oversaw that section all night.

Max approached them with two of the nightly shot specials as they sat down.

"What are those?" Alma's eyes went wide at the pink-and-white concoction.

Will handed her one. "It's called Cupid's Panties. White chocolate liqueur mixed with strawberry cream tequila and topped with whipped cream." It took months of cocktail tasting to come up with something that tasted good, fit the theme, and was easy for the bartenders to mix repeatedly.

Alma smiled at Will. "Good thing I have a sweet tooth. Here's to love."

"To love." He smiled back.

There was no graceful way to take the shot, and both ended up with whipped cream on their faces.

He wanted to lick it off her lips.

That was the point of the shot—so one person would be drawn to the other's mouth, and they would think of kissing... and more. Will didn't know it would work so well on him.

He thought he was above it all.

But he was falling fast for the tricks he had set up to encourage others to fall into someone else's arms.

Alma laughed as he handed her a napkin. He wanted to laugh with her but Will, the nightclub owner, did not laugh.

"I only need one of those," she said. He remembered what she said earlier about being a lightweight.

He eyed the table next to them. A woman Will was sure was a famous rock star and her model girlfriend sat down. He stopped himself from smiling. For opening weekend, he'd sent out invitations to celebrities with any passing relationship to Denver. One of them coming by was a good sign. Eros could be a place where the rich and famous let loose.

Will grabbed a reserved sign and placed it on their table. "Come with me while I walk around." He wasn't sure if she was safer staying in the lounge or following him. The more people who saw her, the greater chance someone would recognize her. With her makeup and new hair, it wasn't as big of a risk as before.

But she'd wonder if he left her to do nothing. She was supposed to be hosting with him. It was in her job description.

"What do you need me to do?" she asked as they walked. She leaned into him so he could hear her.

"I'm going to introduce myself to a few guests, make sure they're having a good time. You only need to be charming."

"I can do that."

They stopped at a table by the edge of the dance floor with four women who appeared to be in their mid-twenties. They wore special wristbands denoting they were social media influencers.

Color coding the different invitations had been Max's brilliant idea.

Will introduced himself, and Alma immediately took over, complimenting the women on their masks. They shared how the tutorials on making them broke their view records.

They loved Alma's makeup, but when they asked for a picture, Alma politely declined without upsetting them. Her ability to charm and disarm was masterful. Will felt superfluous next to her. All he contributed were VIP passes for a future date.

"Are you okay I turned down the picture? Since this is all fake, I don't think either one of us needs those pictures lingering."

He kissed her forehead. "You were amazing." It wouldn't be a lie to tell his mother that Alma didn't let her guard down easily. If he'd insisted, she would pose for the picture. But Alma was right: the less evidence of her being there, the better it would be in the long run.

"If anyone gets a picture of us now, they'll definitely believe we're a couple."

"What?" He stood close to her because of the loud music. Sure.

"Because you're looking at me like I'm vital to your existence," Alma said.

She gave him the same look. But he wasn't a professional actor.

They stopped at a few more tables; Alma's charm grew with each stop. She fell easily into the role of host, something she likely did often if she volunteered for her father's campaign. She'd be able to charm any donor she came across.

"You okay?" He saw her pleasant expression fade when they finished at the fourth group.

"Yes, just thirsty from talking."

"Head to the lounge. I'll catch up with you."

"You sure?"

"Yes, relax a bit and have fun. Just don't forget you're my girlfriend."

"No chance of that." She leaned in and kissed his cheek before walking away. His eyes followed her until she settled.

He was glad she didn't see his face flush at the spot her lips touched.

He waved Max over. "Can you keep an eye on Alma? Make sure she gets water."

"Of course. You should be aware—I've heard from the staff that there've been requests to make ladies' drinks stronger without telling them."

"What?" He had done enough to lower inhibitions, but he didn't want people to think they could violate consent.

"We aren't doing it. We're checking in with the women, and if they don't know the men or don't want the stronger drinks, then the men are being removed and banned."

"Good." He might be the one club that didn't do ladies' night specials. From the years he spent bartending, he knew those deals were less about budget-conscious women and more about getting them drunk so men could take advantage.

That wasn't what he wanted for Eros. He felt protective of Alma over everyone else, but he was responsible for every woman who stepped into his club. This was supposed to be a safe space for people to let loose, all people.

He had to set boundaries for the patrons.

He looked to Alma and saw the rock star had moved tables to join her. She looked like she was holding court. Pride filled him. He wanted this every night with her. For her to be his queen.

He greeted a few more tables then headed to the VIP lounge.

"Will!" Alma exclaimed, then grasped his face in her hands and kissed him. Her lips parted, and she tasted like salt.

He never wanted this to end.

But, as quickly as the kiss started, she pulled away, and he saw her reaction.

She smirked, and his heart fell.

"Are you having fun?" he asked, needing to change the subject.

"I am! You have to meet my new friends." She made introductions, and Max came by with another round of drinks. He intercepted Alma's and tasted it. She glared at him, squishing the lines of her makeup mask together. Once he verified it was water, he handed it to her, and she took a long sip through the cocktail straw.

He put his arm around her shoulders so she was flush against his body.

He kissed the side of her head. "Are you doing okay?" he whispered into her ear.

She faced him. "Yes, I'm sorry. They did shots, and I tried to say no..."

"You're fine. Keep up with the water." He cradled her face in his hand, and she moved into him. A performance. He understood that. Good thing she still looked alert.

But that wasn't the only thing he was concerned with.

He might be going through the motions with his mother's plan, but he didn't put it past her to send someone else to get some compromising pictures.

Alma didn't like being drunk. She never had and was always afraid she'd do something dumb she'd regret the next day.

Like leaning up against Will as if she needed him for balance.

But even with her inebriation, she felt safe. She was protected by Will. And the staff watched out for her. The VIP bouncer, Ben, constantly made eye contact with her to check in. They watched everyone as they were taking extra precautions with her. If she wasn't here with Will, she'd let loose and have fun, and she'd be safe.

"Hey, it's time to go," he said, shifting away from her.

"You don't need to stay until closing?" She didn't wear a watch, and her phone was in her clutch, but it was obvious the party was still going.

"No, it's late enough. I don't have to stay."

"Will, it's opening night. You can't skip out early." This club meant everything to him. She could tell. She hated that he'd miss out because she couldn't hold her alcohol the way he needed her to.

"It's fine. My staff has everything under control. If they need me, I'm right across the street."

"I'm not concerned about the work. This is supposed to be fun for you."

"Let's go home, and then we can have some fun." Will winked.

She smiled. If only. His words were meant for the two other guests at the table.

"I can go. I know I've had too much. You should stay," she said.

His forehead wrinkled. "I go where you go. Is something wrong?"

She hesitated. This would only work if she was honest

with him. "I don't want you to miss out on anything because of me."

"I'm not. You've done wonderfully. But it's time for us to go. Everyone is having fun. My staff has this under control. The one thing I need to do is get you in bed."

Everything he said sounded like the truth to her.

"Okay." She stood, a little unsteady in her heels.

He took her hand and led her through the crowd. Everyone parted as they approached, making their escape easy. It was unclear to her foggy brain if everyone recognized his role as owner or if his confident manner was enough.

She loved being caught in his wake.

Once outside, the cold air hit her. Sweat sat on her skin, and it chilled in the night air.

"Here." Will placed his suit jacket on her shoulders. They'd skipped coats when they left his place since the club was so close, and it was one less thing to keep track of.

"Thank you." She smiled at him and felt warm from the look he returned.

She couldn't tell if he was being polite or if they were still acting or if she had actually charmed him. She didn't like it.

Her fuzzy brain wanted to charm him.

No, she thought. *He is taking care of his employee.* After all, she was sleeping in his bed that night, and he'd be mad if she got sick in it.

Despite the later hour, the street was busy as they walked to catch the crosswalk.

Near the corner, a long line of people stood outside a storefront.

"What's this?" She stopped in the middle of the sidewalk. He stepped back to stay with her.

"Cupcakes," he said with little interest.

"Are they any good?" A cupcake sounded good to her. She didn't normally have a sweet tooth, despite what she said earlier, but the night made her rethink what she assumed about herself.

"I've never tried them. But they were featured on some travel show a few years ago," he said.

"You live and work in the same block, and you've never had the famous food?" She crossed her arms over her chest.

He looked away and shook his head, a wide grin spreading across his face.

She bit her lip to keep herself from smiling. She'd win this fight, and she wouldn't let his handsome face distract her.

She wanted a cupcake.

And to make him smile again.

She figured out a few things about him in the short time she'd known him. He had a public persona and a private one. The public one was serious and impossible to impress. He ran a high-end nightclub with a line around the block. He was changing the entire subculture around it.

Private Will was soft and laughed and would curl up on the couch with a blanket and make sure the woman in his life ate and stayed hydrated.

"Let's get cupcakes," she said. "You can take it out of my wages."

He growled. "I can buy you a cupcake." He grabbed her hand and walked to the front of the line.

"You can't cut in line like this," she protested.

"Yes, I can," he said. He got to the counter while people shouted at him. He plucked a stack of paper from his jacket pocket. "Hi, I'll have the red velvet. She'll have the..."

Alma read the board quickly. "Black and white."

"And here are twenty-five VIP passes to Eros for the customers who have been inconvenienced." He handed the clerk the stack. "Everyone gets a free drink for their trouble."

Alma looked at him in amazement.

She grinned. Being the club owner did have its perks even if he was an insufferable ass about it.

Word traveled through the line of what was happening, and the protests stopped. Most of the people came from the club, and the VIP passes would ensure a return visit and keep them happy.

The cashier handed him a small box with the treats, and he reached for Alma's hand.

"We could've waited in line," she said.

"It's cold and your feet hurt," he said.

She squinted. "How did you know?" She hadn't said anything because she didn't want to complain. No one weighed her needs seriously.

"I guessed. I don't want to waste any time with you out here when you could be home and out of that dress."

She gasped before remembering they were still in public and were supposed to be insufferably in love. He flirted with her because that was expected and nothing more.

It didn't stop her eyes from flicking down to his crotch, and she might have imagined the faint outline of an erection.

He definitely noticed that.

"Walk, my love, or I will carry you home."

For one small moment, she let that fantasy play out in her head. She wasn't opposed to the idea.

Chapter Four

WILL WASN'T ACTING ANYMORE. HE WAS BEYOND flirting with her. He wanted her so badly he kept forgetting to keep his distance and not push things. They'd established rules, and he intended to follow them. Never mind that he wanted to pull her in for a kiss. But he couldn't do that. Not when it meant so much to him and nothing to her. And she didn't know the stakes of the game they played.

He kept his hand in hers until they reached the elevator in his building. It created a line between the real and fake worlds, as he was aching to stay in the fake one.

They crossed the threshold into his apartment and her shoulders immediately rounded.

"Fuck, my feet do hurt," she groaned. It was exactly as he expected. She turned off everything she hid as soon as she was in his place.

He reached to take his jacket from her. He liked having another thing marking her as his. But now, he no longer had a claim to her. "Have a seat at the table." She did and removed her shoes. He adjusted the heat and wondered for a moment if he had a sweater or a pair of wool socks to offer her. Anything to tie her to the space and to him.

He got her a glass of water and sat across from her, handing her the cupcake and a fork.

"Do you always eat in the dark?"

He hadn't turned on any lights besides the one at the main entry.

"No. But you're not allowed to see my face," he said.

There were a few candles on the table the decorator had picked out. He found a lighter, and they provided enough light to see their dessert.

"Better?" he asked.

"Yes," she said and then moaned with a mouthful of cake. "This is so good."

He took a bite of his cupcake. "Damn. I've been missing out." Even though he had moved into the apartment recently, he spent so much time at Eros and never gave the cupcake shop a second look.

She giggled. "Should have brought me in a long time ago."

He didn't know what to say to that.

He noticed she suppressed a smile. She might have been successful, but she was a little drunk.

"What are you thinking about?" he asked.

She blushed. "How do you know I'm thinking about anything besides this cupcake?"

"You're not as difficult to read as you think you are."

She scrunched her eyes together. "It's not an appropriate thought to share with one's employer."

His cock hardened. He wanted her to be thinking about slow sex in the dark and licking frosting off each other. Then the two of them would be thinking the same thing.

"Now you have to tell me."

She gave him a look asking *Do I?*

He kept his eyes on her.

She sighed. "Multiple people asked me if you have sex with your mask on."

Will choked on his cupcake.

"What did you tell them?" he asked after he regained his composure.

"No, obviously. I know exactly what you look like." She winked and then paused for a moment, examining her cupcake. "I like the masks. More than I expected to," she admitted.

He smiled at that. The point was to give people freedom and his vision came through, especially for her. "Good. I'm glad. What else did you like?"

"Everyone did treat me a little differently because I'm your girlfriend, but overall, I felt free from performing like I normally do."

"Even though you were acting?"

She gave him a bit of side-eye. "Are we going to pretend you don't know who my father is?"

"I can if that's what you want." He'd give her anything.

"That's beyond the point. I'm thankful for everything he's done for me. He's given me opportunities and privileges most people don't dream of. But what he wants for me and what I want for me are two different things."

Will was surprised. He hadn't seen any indication Charles Blake was anything other than supportive of his daughter's career, even if it was outside the family's firm. "What do you want?"

She put down her fork. "I shouldn't. You're my boss. We don't have to talk about my problems."

"I can be your friend, too." Warning bells rang in his head. He shouldn't get closer to her, shouldn't bring her into him. It was a fast track to hurting her more.

But he needed her honesty like he needed air.

"I want to act. But I can't do it in Denver much longer.

Other cities have more opportunities. My dad thinks I should go to law school and won't continue to support me financially if I don't. Like every other kid living with their parents, I need to find a way to survive on my own."

"So, you're hanging out with me for the money," he said.

"Absolutely." She wouldn't meet his gaze. "But I'm having fun, too. People won't know me somewhere else. I'd make a name based on my work and not because my father runs things. It'll get worse if he becomes mayor."

The program Will had tucked in his office drawer featured a full-page advertisement for Blake Smith with a large picture of Charles Blake. Alma's cast picture was smaller.

"I saw you in *Midsummer*," he said.

"You did?"

"Yes, closing week. You were fantastic."

"Thank you. I guess that answers the question of how you found me."

"I don't go to the theater often, but I'm glad I did."

"I guess the tiny costume didn't hurt the case for me being your fake girlfriend," she said.

"You could've been in puffed sleeves and miles of fabric and you still would've been magnificent."

He saw her blush even in the dark.

"Thank you."

His chest tightened at the thought of Alma leaving Denver. He couldn't follow her, not when he recently started a business.

Maybe it was for the best. It would be easier to extract her from his head if she was gone, since they had no future anyway.

"This whole fake relationship thing is confusing, right? It's not just me."

He looked up from his cupcake as she said it—a pressure

valve releasing in his mind. It sure confused the hell out of him, and he was the one who'd orchestrated it.

"It is." He'd be honest with her when he could. "You're talented and charismatic, and you'd have chemistry with a boiled potato. But you have a tell."

"A what?"

"A tell. When you are particularly proud of a performance, you smirk."

"I absolutely do not."

"You do. You smirked after you kissed me tonight."

A dozen expressions appeared over her face in a matter of seconds. "That wasn't a smirk. That was a smile! Girlfriends are supposed to smile when they kiss their boyfriends."

"It was a smirk." She'd been pleased with his reaction to her. He wanted the kiss to go on forever. "I'll prove it to you. We'll play poker, and I'll clean you out."

"Maybe you're good at poker."

"I'm terrible at poker. But I can read you, Alma." He kept his voice calm, luxuriating in the idea he had something special with her.

"Fine," she said. "Now that I know, I won't do it again."

"You will. At least for me, you will."

"Because you've asked nicely?"

"Yes."

She shook her head with a smile on her face.

He didn't deserve her trust. He might not be trying to ruin her, but that was how this whole weekend started. If she knew who he was, if she knew who his mother was, she'd leave his apartment and never look back.

ALMA CHANGED INTO A T-SHIRT AND PLAID PANTS. *The opposite of sexy,* she thought. Standing in his bathroom rummaging in her toiletry bag, she realized she didn't bring anything to remove her makeup.

"Shit."

"Everything okay?" One door in the bathroom led to the bedroom and another to the living room area of the apartment. She'd left Will in the kitchen, but he must have been right outside the door if he heard her swear.

"Yes, I forgot makeup remover." The product she normally used for stage makeup was likely sitting on her counter at home.

"Here, let me." The door opened a crack and then shut.

"It's fine. I'm dressed."

"No, it's not that. I don't have my mask on."

She rolled her eyes. The anonymous thing was a gimmick at the club, and she didn't know why he couldn't give it up around her.

"My eyes are closed." The door stayed shut. "You can trust me."

The door opened, and she felt him step in. "I bought some in case this happened."

"Thank you." She heard him open the cabinet and set something on the counter next to her.

Even without the ability to see, she felt the space he occupied. It wasn't a small bathroom, but with the door closed, he was larger than life.

He ran the tap, and it sounded like he was getting a washcloth wet. He stood in front of her, and her heart rate increased.

"May I?" he asked, his fingers barely touching her face.

She nodded, not confident in her voice.

"Hang on, I'm going to have you sit up here so you're at eye level. Hold onto my shoulders." He guided her hands so she gripped him. She shouldn't be noticing how good his muscles felt under the T-shirt he changed into. His hands skimmed her sides, and she bit her cheek to keep her expression neutral. When he reached her hips, he applied enough pressure to lift her and set her on the counter.

He released her as quickly as he touched her. He stepped closer and she shifted her legs to the side so her knee bumped his hip.

"You do this for all your employees?" One of his hands cradled her head while he used the cloth to dab around her eyes.

"Only the ones that sleep in my bed."

"And how many have done that?" she asked. The real question to her was obvious.

Am I special to you?

"Just you. I keep strict boundaries between myself and my regular employees."

Alma was absolute jelly in his hands, melting into him. If he nudged her knees apart, she would let him between them, hoping he'd take his touch farther. But he didn't. Instead, he continued to cleanse her face, being far gentler with her skin than she normally was with herself.

"You're still holding onto me."

"Oops, sorry." She released his shoulders and didn't know what to do with herself. She placed her hands under her thighs as if that would somehow ease the ache between them.

"I wasn't complaining." She thought she heard a smile in his voice.

It was fair, right? If he held her as if she was precious, she could hold onto him like he was her life raft.

He released her abruptly, signaling he was done.

"I'll be gone before you wake up in the morning," he said.

"Thank you," she said. "I know I wasn't exactly a model employee tonight."

"What are you talking about? You were flawless." His

hand was back in her hair, and he gently kissed her forehead. "Get some sleep. I left water on the bedside table."

He exited the room, and Alma gave herself a moment before opening her eyes.

She checked her reflection and saw her skin was completely clean. She touched the spot where he'd kissed her. She didn't know what he thought or what he wanted from her.

So much of her life was spent trying to figure out if people spent time with her because of her father or if they cared about her. She excelled at reading their true intentions. She kept most people at a distance because the odds were skewed toward people wanting connections to her father and not because they wanted her.

She didn't understand Will. He was clear she was an employee, and they were pretending, but even when they were alone, she felt like he cared about her. But he was still hiding something from her, beyond the obvious. She just didn't know what.

Chapter Five

WILL SNUCK OUT OF HIS APARTMENT EARLY THE next morning. As expected, he couldn't sleep knowing Alma was so close to him, and he couldn't reach for her. And, from a practical standpoint, she might be an early riser, and he couldn't chance her walking into the living room and catching him with his mask off.

The more time he spent with her, the more hurtful it would be for her to find out his identity.

He'd never wanted to hurt her, and now he was determined to take care of her.

He wore his mask to his car in the parking garage and only once he was away from the building did he remove it. He drove a few miles from downtown until he got to the apartment complex where he lived.

The apartment was his refuge, the place where he didn't hide. But now, he felt so fractured he didn't feel complete anywhere. He liked his space by the club more and more, as long as Alma was in it. This apartment, the one he lived in for years, now felt empty without her.

He got dressed in a faded pair of jeans and a T-shirt. He

was as unrecognizable in this outfit as he was in a mask. He wondered what Alma would think of his everyday look. The suit fit a part of his personality, but he had depths beyond what she'd seen.

He drove to his parents' house, passed through the gate, and was informed by the household staff they were in the dining room.

"Will! It's so good to see you." His mother rose and embraced him. His father's gaze remained on his paper.

"Morning." He poured himself a cup of coffee.

"Chef prepared waffles. If I knew you were coming, I would have asked him to include you," Judy said.

"I'm fine." He'd grabbed a breakfast burrito at his apartment. He made them in bulk and then froze them, so he always had something to eat. Tomorrow, he'd cook Alma breakfast. Maybe even eat with her.

"How was your night?"

Will kept his gaze neutral. He didn't need to glare at his mother.

"It was fine." Alma had the right idea. It was a big night for him. He should focus on the success of the club and not his mother's schemes.

"How's the girl?" his father Robert asked.

He'd gladly focus all his attention on Alma.

"Woman. And she's great, actually. Smart, beautiful, amazingly talented. She doesn't deserve this," Will said.

Judy shook her head. "What did I say about cold feet?"

"That doesn't even matter. Her defenses are up. That article about her costumes has her worried. She's not going to do anything. She's an absolute professional." He didn't mention the fading spark in Alma's eyes when she thought he was disappointed in her behavior. He was so focused on making sure she was okay, he didn't wonder about her feelings at that moment. The idea that she cared about what he thought did things to him.

He wanted to kiss her in the bathroom last night.

But it could never happen. And if his mother knew he was developing feelings for Alma, she'd turn it into a weapon against him.

"And even if it wasn't a horrible thing to do to someone, and she somehow let her guard down enough, it won't work. The voters won't care if Charles Blake's daughter did cocaine or got drunk at a club."

"They will care. He'll look like a hypocrite."

"How?"

"He just will. If you don't go through with this, I'll pull my funding for your club."

Will stared her down. It was the one thing keeping him in line and stopping him from divulging everything to the press. He didn't intend to lose his club.

But it felt less and less like it mattered. He had other options.

"You've already seen this doesn't work. You got that blog to post about her costumes and everyone defended her." The author suggested her exposed skin was emblematic of the downfall of the American family.

Skin he wanted to taste.

But that wasn't relevant.

The most frustrating part of all this for Will was that his mother didn't believe any of this garbage. She had endorsements from abortion rights groups, but the second her hold on power was threatened, she threw all her feminist ideals out the window. The fact that she walked a line between being a progressive in public and terrible to him in private was something he'd reconciled a long time ago.

"It doesn't have to be one thing. It can be a combination of things," Judy said.

"Are you proud of who you're teaming up with? You know the people behind those blogs don't support you any more than they support Blake. They will turn on you the second they can. And it won't even matter because no one is going to care if she has a good time at a club. Especially if it comes out that she's with me. You're the hypocrite in all of this. Would it truly be so terrible if he won? You used to be friends. Your policies are nearly identical."

"Yes, it would be terrible. I need to consider the whole city. This is about all our futures."

He was done arguing with her. He'd stick with his plan—go through the motions with Alma and convince his mother she was incorruptible.

If he lost the club, he lost the club.

But this was his only chance to be with Alma. He'd be a fool not to use that time to his advantage. He'd give her fond memories of the time they spent together. Because she would hate him if she ever found out the truth.

WHEN ALMA STEPPED INTO EROS THAT NIGHT, SHE had a new appreciation for the space. The music, the bodies, and the drinks all caused the place to feel otherworldly.

The masks.

At first, she thought them a gimmick. Eros could claim it was unique. The obvious catch to her was that they'd lead to reckless behavior and people being creeps when they were anonymous.

Now Alma understood.

If the lights were up, her makeup wouldn't hide her identity, but in the darkness, it gave her freedom. A chance to act out of character. She could be anyone she wanted. Or anyone Will wanted. It was a chance to explore who she was if she wasn't held down by her family's expectations.

Over dinner, she watched him more carefully than the night before. He sat with her, and they ate steak and baked potatoes rivaling any she'd been served in a restaurant.

In the shadows of the apartment, even with his mask on, she thought she saw the real Will. He smiled and laughed, and when she put on the dress he'd picked out for her, he looked at her like she was the sun.

But here at the club, all that was different. His face shielded most of his emotions.

She wished to know what he was thinking but was too afraid to ask. Afraid the answer was something like the fire code and not her. When she was in the real world, she spent a lot of energy watching the reactions of the people she interacted with. Everyone had an agenda with her. She always had her walls up. People saw her first as someone they could get something from. Like she'd advance their career at Blake Smith if they dated her.

It confused the hell out of her that she couldn't tell what Will wanted.

It shouldn't matter. This wasn't the "real Will," and she wasn't the "real Alma."

As they moved to the VIP area, Will's hand rested on her back. The dress she wore was white with an open back that left much skin exposed. When he touched her, there was nothing between them.

She leaned into him, taking all the intimacy that she got. It wouldn't last, and she was fully prepared for an ache at the end of their time together.

That happened with shows sometimes, with particularly good cast mates and a fun role. Even after the weeks of rehearsals and performances, instead of being ready to move on, she'd be bereft after it was over. Like she didn't know who she was without Titania.

That's all that's happening, she told herself.

It was more crowded than it had been the night before. Word must have spread, and since it was Friday, more people could have a night out.

Max arrived almost as soon as they sat down. They repeated the ritual from the previous night—taking a shot of something tequila-based, and Alma offered they toast to the fantasy.

She bit her lip as she said it, wondering if she was showing her cards. How would he react if he thought she was throwing herself at him?

He smiled, and she'd do almost anything to be the object of that smile.

They sat next to each other, continuing their conversation from dinner. He asked about the auditions she was preparing for, and which Shakespeare production was her favorite. He was easy to talk with and since the club was loud, they had to keep their faces close.

She was aware they weren't doing what they were supposed to be doing. She wasn't making the VIPs feel special. He wasn't being the charming host.

She didn't think either one of them cared.

She hadn't noticed when Max returned until Will kissed her temple possessively, and his attention turned to the server.

"I'm really sorry. I know you said you're not working exactly, but the internet cut out for a second, and we can't get in without the administrator password," she said.

"Fuck." He squeezed Alma's thigh as he stood up. "I'll be back as soon as I can."

She reached for the hand that lit her skin on fire and held it.

"Hurry. I want to spend time with you." It sounded desperate to her ears.

He leaned forward and briefly touched his lips to hers. "Soon." She parted her lips to deepen the kiss, but he pulled away.

She hated the loss of him.

Knowing she was exposed, she called up all her acting skills and smirked.

Some emotion she couldn't read flashed in Will's eyes before he walked away.

Max took his place. "You're doing a number on him."

Alma shook her head. "You know this is all fake."

"I've worked with that man for years. I know him. He's not acting."

"Maybe, but I am." She bit the inside of her lip to stop reacting.

"Are you?"

Alma didn't respond.

"What else can I get you?" Max picked up the empty shot glasses.

"Um, water. I'm not feeling great from last night, and I want to take it easy tonight," Alma said. "I need to be a good employee."

"I'll bring you a vodka bottle filled with water and some mixers. Then it looks like you have bottle service, and no one will question it."

"That sounds great, thanks."

Max stood up. "I'll be right back. Keep your eye on your drink. People will be shady if they see an opportunity. But if you need anything, grab Ben over there." She gestured to the bouncer.

"Thanks."

She told herself to give everything she had to the next few

hours with Will. She could play the ideal social girlfriend to the club owner.

It was method acting, she'd say if asked.

She would deal with the consequences on Sunday when she returned to her real life.

Max brought her the water and mixers, and Ben walked over to say hi. He made the same comment about Will being less of a grump since she came into the picture. She smiled and shrugged, hoping it was a vague enough gesture for him to interpret whatever suggestive way he wanted.

She wasn't alone very long when a man and two women joined her. She didn't catch their names but decided to smile along with their conversation. She wanted to wait by herself for Will, but she was getting paid to entertain the guests, and so she would. The three of them wore masquerade masks hiding most of their faces, each with more beading and embellishment than the last. She could be sitting in front of people she saw every day and wouldn't know.

Max got their drink orders and gave Alma a look telling her to flag her down if there were any issues. She sipped her ice water with lime and let herself enjoy the company around her. An edge went up around her like she needed to watch for something, but she didn't know what. She hadn't felt this Thursday night.

But she pushed it down and instead focused on the chatter. They were visiting Denver and couldn't imagine missing the opening of Eros. Alma shared that she was dating the owner, and they were very excited to hear that.

In her real life, she would've been annoyed they were interested in her for her connections. But when it was her relationship with Will, she felt proud of it. She wanted to be attached to him. To be someone to show off.

Her guard eased down.

She was about to wave Max over to get an alcoholic drink

when one woman pulled out a small baggy from her purse. She placed it discreetly on the table. "Let's kick this party up a notch."

Alma sat frozen for a moment. Will hadn't talked to her about this, and she didn't want to do drugs.

Before Alma could react, a hand grabbed her upper arm and jerked her away. She saw Ben approach the people at the table.

Will dragged her out of the VIP area and down a hallway away from the loud music.

Anger radiated off him.

"I didn't do anything; I swear." She sucked in a breath at the thought he was mad at her.

He stopped walking, and she backed herself against the wall. He held her face in both his hands. "Are you okay? Do you feel dizzy or anything?" His eyes scanned hers.

It took her a moment to realize Will thought they might have put something in her drink. "No. I'm fine. My drink was in my hand the whole time."

"Good." Then he pressed his lips to hers.

This time, he parted her mouth and sought out her tongue with his. Her hands went to his back, tugging him against her. She felt his hard arousal against her stomach as their mouths devoured each other. One of his hands drifted down until it reached her hip, and he pulled her close to him.

Chapter Six

SHE WAS HEAVEN IN WILL'S ARMS. HER LIPS WERE soft, and he felt her strength and desire as she embraced him.

He hadn't been sure he'd be able to get to her fast enough. Max told him a group asked her to point out the owner's girlfriend, and he knew it wasn't a coincidence. Not a request that specific. A thousand terrible thoughts had rushed through his head. They could have put something in her drink. Or staged a photo to look like she was doing something more risqué than she was.

It never occurred to him that they would go straight to cocaine.

His mother crossed a line.

Will broke the kiss. He couldn't cross a line.

Kissing her where no one could see, because he needed her safe and to pour his emotions into her, wasn't a part of the plan.

He removed his hand from her hip and placed it on the wall next to her head.

He was breathing hard.

She was breathing hard.

"I'm sorry, I—"

"No, it's fine." She leaned against the wall, but not to put distance between them, since she still held onto him. "We agreed this is confusing. I told you I'd tell you if you went too far." She paused a moment as if to collect herself. "So, what was that?" She gazed down to where their bodies touched—his erection obvious to her.

Holding her close like this was the one way he could cherish and protect her. She was only his for a short time. "I reacted. I shouldn't have kissed you."

She cut him off. "I know what the kiss was. I want...I mean, kissing you isn't a hardship." She flushed.

Her hands rested on his chest. He wrapped an arm around her waist and with the thumb of his other hand, he gently traced her lip.

She hadn't smirked. This was real.

"Or something that you're acting through?" he offered.

"I..." She didn't finish her sentence, and he wondered if she was afraid to show too much of herself.

He cradled her jaw in his hand and rested his forehead on hers. "You're not alone."

She let out a deep breath. "What were you reacting to?"

"They had cocaine, and who knows what else. Ben and the rest of security will deal with them."

"I wasn't going to do it. Even if it was my thing, I'm on the clock. I wouldn't risk your reputation."

"What does my reputation have to do with anything?" He didn't understand why she was focused on him when she could have been hurt.

"I'm guessing it'd be bad press if your girlfriend was caught doing drugs. Unless that's what you want, but I won't agree to that."

Will paused the motion of his hand. He saw sincerity in her eyes and how she cared more about his reaction than the consequences for her. He wondered what her father's reaction had been to the article about her costumes, if he told her it was her fault they got negative attention. He wondered if she spent her whole life making sure she had a perfect outward appearance, so her skills and talents reflected positively on Charles Blake, if he threatened her if she stepped out of line.

"I don't care about my reputation or my club if you get hurt in the process. I care those fuckers got close enough to you that security had to intervene. Nothing you do is about me. Your choices are your own. You are your own person." He struggled to maintain control of his voice. He was angry. But not at her, and he didn't want her to think he was.

She trembled under his touch. "I know that. But I'm still your employee."

He tried to pull away, but her fingers dug into his shirt, keeping him in place. Her eyes scanned his, and he required distance between them. He couldn't be this close to her and hold so much from her.

He wanted to tell her she was more than that to him. That she was quickly becoming someone whose presence he needed to feel like himself, whose scent made him feel at home.

But he couldn't tell her that. Not when she was leaving in a day. But he could tell her something else.

"You're not Charles Blake's daughter to me."

Her breath caught.

"You're Alma," he continued. "A smart, talented woman who's so beautiful I can't look at you too long or I'll burn up."

Her eyes tracked between his for a few seconds before she closed the distance between them and kissed him.

Fuck, he needed her in his life. He trailed kisses down her neck.

"Wait," she said.

He pulled back.

"Something else is going on here. Tell me."

He held a hand in each of his and kissed her knuckles. He spaced them so their hands were their only point of contact.

"I had a meeting with my investor today," he said. "It didn't go well."

She tensed.

"I'm on edge, and I didn't realize how much I needed you here. For me."

"Is that why I'm here? For you?" She rubbed the backs of his knuckles with her thumbs. The touch sent jolts of sensation through him.

"Yes." It was the truth. He was being completely selfish with her, taking her comfort when he had nothing to offer in return.

"What happens when this weekend is over?"

"You'll go home, and I'll never see you again," he said. He hated that thought even more now.

"Why?"

He couldn't meet her eye because he had no good reason why he couldn't be with her.

He should tell her everything. Who he was and why she was specifically hired to be by his side all weekend. And how people might try to hurt her father through her. Fuck, he should remove his mask, kiss her senseless, and tell her he needed her.

But then she'd walk out and never forgive him. He wasn't ready for that. He'd hold onto her a little longer.

Her eyes searched his. She wasn't faking this interaction. Her need for his touch was as real as his. He didn't know if it was a physical attraction or something more. But he wasn't alone in this.

He needed more time with her.

The door to the hall opened. "We're all clear, sir," Ben said.

"Thank you." He wasn't ready to let Alma go. "We should head in."

"Of course." She removed herself from his embrace. "Makeup okay?"

"It's perfect."

She smiled and then smirked.

But he saw the effort she put into it.

"I'll be by your side the rest of the night. I promise nothing will happen to you." He interlaced his fingers with hers.

"What happens when I have to pee?"

He laughed. "You think I won't stand outside the door glaring at everyone who comes by? I brought you here. It's my responsibility to protect you."

She laughed, but it sounded forced.

WHEN THEY RETURNED, THE LOUNGE WAS EMPTY. It wouldn't be long before the VIPs filtered in, but he reveled in a last moment alone with Alma.

He tucked a strand of hair behind her ear. "You okay to keep going? We can head to my apartment and call it a night." The urge to tell her this was fake hadn't dissipated. She had to see through him.

"I'm fine. I can do this. Masks up, right?"

He thought it would feel better knowing she was as attracted to him as he was to her, but it led to more pain for both of them.

"Masks up," he repeated. The hallway was real. The club was fake. They had an understanding.

They sat at the same table from earlier. All the drinks had been cleared, and Alma's clutch lay discarded in a chair.

"Sorry, I should've grabbed that. I wasn't thinking."

"It's fine. It's just my phone." She pulled out a tube of lipstick and a mirror.

"Now I know not to use smudging your lipstick as an excuse not to kiss you."

"You definitely have some on you...and we can see about rubbing it off on some other part of you later."

She finished and looked at him with a straight face. As if the idea of her mouth on his dick was completely normal.

Then she smirked and burst out laughing. "I'm sorry, I tried, but your face."

He laughed with her. "Fuck, Alma. You can't do that to me."

"I know. Everything got so serious, and I had to break the tension. You would date someone who would say suggestive things about blow jobs."

"Would I?" The only person he wanted to date was Alma.

She gestured around them. The lounge was filling up again, and he absorbed the scene of the club.

"Anyone you date would have to know exactly who they are to keep up with this. So yes, they would be incredibly confident about their skills in bed, and they wouldn't be ashamed."

"You've given this a lot of thought."

"Of course. It's my job."

"Do you, Alma, know exactly who you are?"

She looked surprised he asked. But the question was obvious to him.

"I'm an actor. I can be whomever you desire."

Max interrupted them. Will suppressed his annoyance for all the interruptions. "Sorry, we had to take everything away. But I can get you a new bottle."

"How much have you had to drink?" He'd noticed a bottle of vodka on the table earlier.

"The one with you. I was drinking water and mixers."

He kissed her temple. "How about we get a bottle of champagne?" He wanted to spoil her.

"What are we celebrating?" She looked at him through her eyelashes, and he thought of spending the rest of the night making her eyes roll back into her head with pleasure.

"I'm always celebrating you."

She smiled. "That's very cheesy. You should be careful, Will. You'll lose your reputation as a very serious club owner."

"She's right," Max said. "Staff thinks you've gone soft. If she sticks around, we'll take advantage and unionize."

"Go ahead. Unionize. Just bring me champagne."

Max snickered and headed to the bar.

Come Sunday, Alma's leaving will gut him. But after his deception, there was no future together for them anyway. If they met in the real world, she'd recognize him instantly. He hadn't done anything to disguise his voice. The mask only hid so much.

The election was in six weeks.

He couldn't stand next to his mother on election night or any other occasion ever again. He imagined the betrayal Alma would experience seeing him there. She'd know he used her, and he couldn't hurt her like that. He would have nothing to do with his family if it meant keeping Alma safe and not knowing what he'd done.

Max returned, poured their drinks, and they toasted.

He needed to kiss her. He envisioned himself reaching for her and threading his fingers through her hair. She'd lean into him, and he'd spend the rest of the night learning how she tasted. He could do it. She agreed to that level of intimacy with him, and she'd come close to admitting that she wanted him. But this pushed it too far. Because he knew the stakes of the game she played, even if she didn't.

As the lounge got crowded, a few people joined their table. A look crossed Alma's face he couldn't read. She was deep in thought as she sipped her champagne. He grew concerned that something was wrong.

"Why don't we play a drinking game?" she asked the group before he said anything.

Where had this come from?

Everyone at their table perked up. Alma's posture was straight and her eyes clear. She played expertly into the role he'd hired her for. She outlined the rules to a game he'd never heard of, and they began.

After a few rounds, he was having more fun than he had in a while, and Alma was the center of attention—the picture-perfect image of a nightclub owner's girlfriend.

After one particularly intense round, he turned to her. "You doing okay?" He punctuated the question with a kiss on her temple. A part of him hated forcing her into this role that wasn't her. He wanted to call it off and let her be who she really was.

"Fine." She turned to him and placed her lips on his. "The rules are rigged so you and I rarely drink," she whispered.

She was right. They sipped champagne, but neither drank from the group cup or took a shot.

He leaned in and enveloped her in a kiss.

She laughed and pulled away, exposing her smirk.

"That smirk better be for your gaming skills and not for faking that kiss," he growled in her ear.

She turned again and kissed him. "I'm not smirking now."

"We're going to give you two some privacy," a tablemate said, his group shifting away.

Will was nearly on top of her. His erection hadn't gone down since the hallway. She had to feel it against her thigh.

"Actually, we're heading home. Ready, my love?" He stood and offered his hand to her. She accepted, and they headed to the door.

Leaving with her wasn't a terrible idea. In the sterile environment of his apartment, he would be able to cool his libido. Alma would fall out of character, and he wouldn't be allowed to kiss her anymore.

It was all for the best.

ALMA KNEW WILL WAS THROWING COLD WATER ON them by leaving the club. To anyone else, it was counterintuitive since his bed was a few feet away, and Alma was minutes from crawling under his sheets.

But it made sense to Alma. Outside of the club, she wasn't expected to fawn over him, wasn't expected to flirt with him. He was her boss and nothing more. Those were the rules.

It was for the best. It didn't matter what happened in the hallway. He was clear their relationship ended on Sunday.

Alma didn't date much. For most of her life, she was focused on rehearsals and performing. It didn't leave room for finding a partner outside the theater. And dating someone involved in a production lead to drama, *real* drama.

Enough people tried to get close to her because they thought she would get them in the door at Blake Smith. She couldn't count the number of times she'd been at a bar and someone approached her to buy her a drink, then asked if she could get their resumé to the top of the pile.

Even the few boyfriends that initially had been in it for her, ended up wanting to get close to power. There was one she particularly liked who'd come home with her for Easter. She didn't know he'd been accepted to law school and he spent the entire trip asking Charles how he could best stand out.

After that, she didn't let her guard down.

Then there was Will. When he told her he didn't care about her father, she believed him.

She thought she finally understood what was going on with him. He let her see the man behind the mask. From what few facts she knew about him, she knew who he was behind all the protections he put up. He wanted her, but for whatever reason, wouldn't let himself have her. But somehow, he let his walls come down for her.

She shouldn't trust Will. He was hiding something from her, and when he had the chance to tell her, he didn't. She trusted his actions even if he omitted information. There was more to the story than her playing host for him. Or him needing her for support all weekend. She didn't doubt he wanted that. But she was sure he wanted her specifically and not any actor he came across. Some other game was happening, and she didn't know what piece she was playing. There had to be some reason why he was so certain they'd never see each other again.

But that night taught her one thing: she was safe in Will's arms. It was a balm to the ache she felt at losing him.

They crossed the threshold into his apartment, and she fell into her new role.

What she felt for him, what she did with him, was all real.

There wasn't any hiding. She would remove her mask. His stayed on. They would both pretend like she was simply an actor paid for a job, and the club was the stage.

She stepped away from the door and removed her shoes.

"Those more comfortable than last night?"

"A little. There's no winning with heels." She understood why she needed a different dress every night, but she didn't get why he bought her a different pair of shoes for each night as well. It's not like anyone would notice.

But maybe he wanted to spoil his fake girlfriend.

He removed his suit jacket and moved around the kitchen, getting them both a glass of water.

"Do you want help with your makeup again?"

"No, I can manage." She went to the bedroom and grabbed a clean pair of pajamas before hiding in the bathroom. She let out a deep breath. He was so calm and collected, and she sweated through everything on her body. It would've been comforting to accept his help, to be held a little longer.

She changed out of her dress and hung it on the door. She took her time removing her makeup, hoping to regain some self-control. When she was satisfied she got everything, she opened the door. "I'm coming out."

"Okay, I'm still masked."

She could have exited the other side and gone directly into the bedroom. But she needed one more minute with him.

"I wanted to say thanks for everything tonight," she said.

He looked at her from where he was setting up his bed on the couch, completely confused. She was grateful he was still in his suit. She wouldn't be able to keep him at arm's length if she saw him in casual clothes. "Of course," he said.

"Well, good night."

"Good night. I'm going to shower quickly. I'll try to be quiet."

"It's fine. I'm exhausted. I'll be asleep before my head hits the pillow."

"Good night, Alma. I'll see you tomorrow afternoon."

In the bedroom, she hid under the sheets of his king-sized bed and tried not to imagine water dripping over his naked back. But then she was thinking about it and the way his tongue felt on her skin. Heat pooled between her legs. She wondered how long he would be. She itched to reach into her panties and give herself the orgasm she'd never get from him. She could do it quietly, and the shower would cover any sound she'd make.

Her hand drifted down, but quicker than she expected, the shower turned off. A moment later, the bathroom door opened.

She let out a small squeak.

"Sorry," he whispered.

"I'm awake. It's fine. My eyes are closed," she said.

"I need to grab something from the closet."

"Sure."

She listened to him move around. *He's probably in a towel,* she thought.

She bit her lip and then decided to go for it.

"Hey, Will?"

"Yes, Alma."

"The couch can't be comfy." In for a penny, in for a pound.

"No, Alma." She didn't know if he agreed with her statement about his sleeping arrangement or if he was telling her not to bother with her question. She wasn't done with him for the night. She wanted more answers and to prove to him that she was safe with him.

"Don't let me chase you out of your bed. It's big enough for both of us."

It was dark, she wasn't facing him, and her eyes were closed, but in her mind, he was torn about this decision.

He muttered under his breath.

"I keep a sleep mask in my nightstand. I'll put it on you."

"Okay." She sat up with her eyes closed, and he shuffled to the other side of the bed. The mattress shifted as he moved next to her. He smelled clean, like sandalwood and fresh linen.

He placed the soft mask over her eyes. "Cozy?"

"Yes." It smelled faintly of him. She'd take any closeness she could get.

She got comfortable as he did the same. Sharing a bed with

him felt as intimate as anything else they'd done, even if there was space between them.

"Is it so important that I don't know who you are?"

She read the details of her contract. She wasn't allowed to ask him who he was or to see his face. Asking why was not against the rules.

She was justified in at least asking since his kisses tore her apart.

Even if there was a chance he wouldn't tell her the truth.

"I don't get to be who I am because of who my family is. The mask allows me to be free." It sounded like a real reason. But she knew better. The pretense only stopped when he was alone with her.

"What happens if I decide to come back to Eros next weekend?" she asked.

The silence between them felt like it lasted forever.

"We'll break up amicably. You'll be on the VIP list for life."

"Really?"

"Yes. But I'll be unavailable every time you're there."

Her stomach twisted, hurt at how easily he set her aside.

She wished she could ask him why they couldn't explore what was blooming between them. Why was he so insistent she not know who he was? He was ruining things by not giving them a chance.

She knew he felt the same as she did. Yes, there was attraction, but it was more than that, too. She liked talking with him over dinner and sharing in small conspiracies like the drinking game.

But if he wouldn't answer her tonight, she wasn't going to force it.

It wasn't like she'd go to the club—not if it meant she wouldn't see him. But it could be a fun card to hold in her pocket for parties with friends. She'd come back and remember one weekend when she meant something to him.

She pushed the thought away. No amount of clout with her friends would be worth the loneliness without him.

Not when he was starting to feel like her whole world.

She waited for him to say something, to indicate he was as moved by this as she was. That he'd miss her in his bed when she was gone.

But all she heard was the sound of their breathing.

Chapter Seven

ALMA STIRRED WHEN WILL'S ALARM WENT OFF ON Saturday morning. He kissed her cheek and told her to go back to sleep.

When she woke on her own, she reached for him. His side was cold.

Noise drifted in from the kitchen, so she removed the sleep mask and grabbed her phone.

ALMA

I'm awake, FYI.

WILL

Thanks. I'll be out of here in a few minutes.

I made you French toast. It's in the oven
keeping warm.

ALMA

You didn't have to do that.

WILL

I wanted to.

Did you sleep okay?

ALMA

Yeah, you?

WILL

I did. Thank you.

I'm headed out. I'll see you later.

ALMA

Bye.

She heard the front door close and waited a moment before getting up. She made the bed, holding his pillow to her nose for a moment.

In the kitchen, she found a half pot of coffee and got the French toast out of the oven. He'd left a note, too, clearly written before she woke up.

> *Alma,*
> *I'll be gone all day. If you need anything, give me a*
> *call.*
> *Will*

His handwriting was elegant, but if she was looking for any more insight into who he was, it wasn't there. But she liked living in this fantasy. They were together, and he made her breakfast every morning. He left love notes all over the apartment for her to find.

After she ate and showered, her phone beeped with the unmistakable tone of an incoming video call. One glance at the screen indicated it was her eldest sister, Rachel.

Alma scrunched her face. She wasn't expecting a call and was annoyed the three of them had long ago established the expectation that most calls were video chats. It might have started because of nosiness or being overprotective or because they were constantly asking for outfit advice. Since they were kids, Alma looked up to her sisters. She respected their opinions, but she couldn't answer the call and keep her location a secret.

The ringing eventually stopped, and Alma was drafting a text stating she was unavailable when a second video call came in, this one from her middle sister, Kayla.

She meant to reject that call, too, and add Kayla to the excuse text, but she tapped the wrong button and both sisters' faces appeared.

"Oh, so you pick up for Kayla, but not me." Alma was mostly sure Rachel's outrage was fake. The two of them were attorneys and highly competitive, but they didn't normally compete for Alma's attention.

"I didn't get to my phone in time," she said. She was really in this now.

"Where are you?" Kayla asked. "We swung by the house, and Dad said you were out, but he didn't say more." Both sisters wore campaign shirts.

The family gave up their free time for his campaign. That was the expectation—they were either working or volunteering.

It was one of the reasons her father was annoyed at her taking this job. She wasn't allowed a life outside of him.

She couldn't tell them the truth, not with the NDA Will made her sign, so she settled on a version close to what they were telling at the club.

Alma forced her features into a blush. "I met a guy. I'm at his place."

"How does that get you out of election work?" Rachel asked.

"Ignore her; tell us everything," Kayla said.

They were both married to lawyers. Rachel met her husband in law school, and they both started at Blake Smith when they graduated. Kayla married the man she shared an office with while they studied for the bar. A seating arrangement, they had all suspected, designed by their father with the hopes they'd hit it off. It worked.

They knew Alma didn't date much, that she didn't let new people in. They'd sat with her while she cried over one guy after another who wanted the firm and not her, and how she'd sworn off anyone who made even passing remarks about a legal career.

"It's not a big deal. I met him at a coffee shop a few weeks ago. We're taking things slow, but his nightclub opens this weekend, and he wanted me here while all that was happening."

She was Will's emotional support actor.

"That's so exciting! What's the name of the place? Do you even like clubbing?" Kayla asked. "What's he like?"

"Club Eros. I hadn't been to many. But it's been fun. I'm more observing and entertaining people than anything else."

"Interesting. I'm jealous you got out of campaigning," Rachel said. She had fallen away from the screen and spoke as if distracted. Alma had to guess she was looking up the club on her phone. "Wait, it says you have to wear a mask. Is it a sex thing?"

"No! It's like a masquerade ball, except modern. It's a lot of fun. No one knows who I am."

"Imagine that," Rachel deadpanned.

"I've done mine with makeup. It's really fun." She sent them a picture from Friday night that she snapped in Will's bathroom before they headed out.

"You look like you stepped out of a fairytale!" Kayla said.

"What's your boyfriend's name?"

"Will," Alma said, a little too fast. She liked thinking of him as her boyfriend.

"Last name?"

"Um..."

"You don't know his last name?" Rachel asked. She paused her search to stare at Alma.

"I do. He's private, and we're not ready to go public yet, so I'd rather you not cyberstalk him." That sounded like a plausible solution.

"Never mind, the club tagged him. I have his profile," Rachel said. Alma didn't even know he had social media. It wasn't something she needed to know. They weren't dating. They weren't continuing this relationship past the weekend. It'd be over in less than twenty-four hours. "Is he hot? You can't see his face in any of the pictures."

"Yes, he's hot."

"Can you send us a picture of him? We want to judge for ourselves," Kayla said.

"I don't have one." They accepted that enough. It was a new relationship after all.

"Can we meet him?" Rachel asked.

"He's at work right now. Maybe in a few weeks, once things settle." Her stomach churned. Things wouldn't settle. "Like I said, it's not serious. We're having fun."

Both sisters gave Alma their full attention. "So, you're alone in the apartment of a guy you just met, and it's not serious?" Rachel said.

"What's weird about that?"

"I didn't leave Caleb alone in my apartment until we had been dating for six months," Kayla said. "You've snooped, right?"

"No, that's an invasion of privacy."

"Clearly, but you already said you don't know him that well, and he left you there. It's expected you'll peak in his drawers," Rachel said.

Alma looked around. The place was so generic she wondered if it was staged. There wasn't any privacy to violate.

She shook her head out of the fantasy. Will wasn't her

boyfriend. He was her boss, and he had left her alone in his apartment for two days. He didn't tell her much about him. Did he think she wouldn't look around? Especially after kissing and sleeping in the same bed?

"It's fine. He'll be back soon."

She wasn't sure either sister bought the lie. She was a professional actor, but everyone around her was an expert at reading her lies.

"Maybe we can all go to the club after the election? For a celebration," Kayla suggested.

"Oh god, it's been so long since we've done anything fun like that," Rachel groaned.

"Maybe, that'll be fun," Alma said.

"We have to go since *we* still have responsibilities," Rachel said.

"I'll be around tomorrow," Alma said.

Both sisters waved their goodbyes, and she ended the call.

Will couldn't fault her if she poked around a little. Humans were curious. He was so cautious. What were the chances she'd find something?

She wanted to trust him. His actions toward her screamed she could trust him. But he wouldn't tell her his name or let her see his face. She didn't know what, but maybe there was something in the apartment to give her a hint about what was happening.

The kitchen was the least personal space in any home, so she started there. She moved to the living room, bathroom, and closet. Nothing revealed anything about him that she didn't already know. He was wealthy and spent money on his appearance. But there were no personal items.

He must have recently moved in. Someone couldn't occupy a space and accumulate so little clutter.

In the bedroom, she stared at the nightstand. He'd pulled an eye mask from it the night before, but she had specifically avoided looking in it. People put their secrets in the nightstand.

Could she take this step?

"Fuck it." She hadn't found anything so far, and she didn't think she'd find anything here.

In the drawer, she found a copy of *Romeo and Juliet* and a spare phone charger.

The book was dogeared halfway through the first act.

She put it down and closed the drawer.

WILL PAUSED OVER HIS CHECKLIST FOR THE TENTH time and glanced at his watch. He expected Alma to return from the salon soon, and everything needed to be perfect for his last night with her.

He'd set the table with wine and water glasses and arranged the plates carefully. His mother would've chided him for not using a tablecloth, but he didn't own one. He did, however, buy a new candle with a scent that reminded him of Alma.

It was something for Will to hold onto after she left him.

It had been a mistake to spend the night in his bed with her, even if he kept his hands to himself. Now he'd always know what she looked like sleeping next to him.

His phone buzzed with a message from her. She was headed to him. He changed quickly from his casual clothes and into his suit before putting on his mask. Tonight would be memorable. It was their last chance to let the myth stand. In the remaining few moments, he placed the food on the table.

He'd roasted a whole chicken, with crispy skin he'd expertly carved. He'd contemplated waiting until she arrived to slice it and impress her with his knife skills, but sometimes it was messy, and he didn't need to ruin the atmosphere.

It could have been fun though. Her helping him remove his shirt because he forgot to put an apron on. Them forgetting the food altogether.

He shook his head. Another life.

He also made a creamy pasta with pine nuts and a salad. Everything was from scratch, and he'd spared no effort. If this didn't amaze her, he didn't know what would. It almost didn't matter to him. This was how he took care of her and showed her that she was important to him.

The door opened, and a moment later, Alma stepped into the kitchen.

"Wow. This is elaborate."

Will couldn't speak.

He had woken up next to her that morning. Even with her eyes covered and her face half buried in his pillow, she was stunning and looked like she belonged. He forced himself out of bed because he didn't want her waking up and seeing his face or the look of horror she'd undoubtedly have when she saw him being such a creeper.

He barely understood why she'd offered the bed to him. He hoped it was because she craved his closeness the way he did hers. He'd kicked himself for not having a spare pair of lounge pants already set out for him, forcing him to go into the bedroom. When she was still clearly awake, he knew he wouldn't be able to deny her anything.

When he returned to the apartment after getting groceries, he timed it incorrectly, and she had been on her way out. She offered to help with his bags, but he wanted the meal to be a surprise.

But that set off a new wave of fantasies of running errands with her.

"Will," she said, snapping him back to the moment.

"Sorry, what?"

"Everything okay? You're staring."

So he was.

She wore black leggings and an oversized button-up top. It looked like it could have been stolen from a boyfriend, but she didn't have one. Did she buy it herself? What did she wear when she wasn't performing or auditioning for jobs? He found himself needing to know everything about her life.

She styled her hair like the previous days—loose waves that were supposed to appear effortless.

He'd changed his mind about her makeup at the last minute. Instead of an elaborate design to fulfill the mask requirement, he had asked for a simple smoky eye. She'd be wearing a lace mask, one that hid her identity more than the makeup and kept her protected.

It was also sexy as all hell.

The result of the change was Alma now looked like she was ready for a regular night out. He could be taking her out on a date.

This could be his real life.

He broke away from the fantasy. "Sorry, you look stunning." He ushered her to the table. "We should eat before it gets cold."

"Thanks. Did you make all this? You didn't have to go to so much trouble." She sat while he poured them both wine.

"Your mask is right there." Next to her place was a black box. She opened it to reveal the detailed mask he had picked out. "It'll be comfortable. We'll put it on right before we leave."

"It's beautiful." Her fingers brushed over the design. "You could take yours off, and then we'd have a normal meal." This time, he was aware his entire body stilled. Alma noticed it, too. "I don't want to ask for that, but I am."

"You've been far more trusting and understanding than I

merit." He held onto her faith in him as if it was the only way he was connected to her.

They watched each other for a moment. He could spend the rest of his life staring into her eyes.

"I know you're lying to me. Or not telling me the whole truth. I didn't care when I accepted this job, but now I do. I wish you trusted me."

She shouldn't. He had agreed to a plan to hurt her. It didn't matter he wasn't following through.

Maybe he could tell her. Tell her who he was and what his mother forced him to do. How she was holding his business hostage. Promise her the kisses they shared were real, and he wanted a future with her if she forgave him.

Her life would take her from Denver, and he might not be able to follow. But he wanted the chance to try.

But it was too late for any of that.

"I do trust you," he said. "But this isn't purely about you and me, unfortunately." He decided to focus his attention on his plate rather than getting any more bad ideas.

"Right. I knew it. You're the twin brother of a famous movie star."

"What? No."

He looked up from his plate and saw the smirk on her face.

"Your father is a murderer, and you look exactly like he did when he committed his crimes."

He laughed. "How many of these did you come up with?"

"A fair amount. I had time on my hands today. I notice you didn't deny the last one."

"No murderers in my family that I know of. I promise you, it's both less exciting and more exciting than you think."

"That's not helpful at all." She laughed dryly, and his tension eased. He reminded himself to stay focused on the moment. This was his last night with her, and he wouldn't let it pass with any regrets.

"We should eat before it gets cold," he repeated.

He liked being around her. That was the hardest part. He wanted to take off his mask and have a normal conversation with her. If things were different, he could have asked her out. Eventually, she'd move in, and he'd help her run lines while he cooked.

This plan proved to be the biggest mistake of his life. He'd have her however she'd let him for one more night, and then he'd never see her again.

Chapter Eight

WILL STOOD BEHIND ALMA, TYING ON HER MASK, careful to not tangle her hair.

"Do you have a spouse and kids somewhere?"

"No." He moved her hair to the side and trailed kisses down her neck.

She shivered in his arms.

"We're not in public," she said, leaning into him.

It was a question. *Is this real?*

He needed to know if she was as affected by this relationship as he was. He thought she was. He knew her well enough at this point that he was certain he could tell when she played a role and when she was sincere.

But if he was wrong... If it turned out he was the one being played...

No, that wasn't possible. They'd established communication rules. She would never let it get this far if it wasn't real for her.

He finished with her mask and then stepped around to face her.

He held out his left hand. "Here, no ring tan line, no indention on the skin. I'm faithful in any relationship." He had little to offer her, but he had fidelity.

"Kissing while acting doesn't count," she said. She dared him to challenge her and admit none of it was an act to him.

He'd be wrecked when the weekend ended.

But she continued without forcing the issue.

"You could be really twisted about this. This whole thing could be much bigger than you're letting on," Alma said. Her fingers circled where a wedding ring would rest.

"That's a lot of work when I can tell you the truth," he said. "At least about that."

She thought for a moment. He paid her to not ask questions. She told him originally she was fine with that, but things changed.

He owed her the truth, but it would ruin everything. He'd give her tonight. She'd leave in the morning. Maybe he'd reach out in a few weeks and explain everything. They might still have a chance at happiness.

"You okay?" she asked.

Her fingers slipped, but he held on.

"Yes, sorry." He released her.

"Great, well, I'm ready to go."

She turned to move away from him, but he caught her around the waist. Her eyes widened in surprise, but she eased into his touch. "You don't need to act when it's the two of us."

"I'm not," she said.

He leaned in, giving her a chance to tell him to stop. Instead, she closed her eyes and pressed into him.

His lips gently brushed hers at first, waiting for her reaction. Her hands slid to his neck and she pulled him in closer, her lips parting enough to let his tongue trace hers.

But just as quickly, she moved away.

"Sorry," he said.

"No, that was me. But unless things changed, we should probably go," she said. She didn't bother to mask the disappointment in her voice.

"You're right." He wanted to stay.

He opened the front door for her and stepped into the corridor. When he locked the door behind them, she reached for his hand. He smiled.

"Let's have fun. I'm only your girlfriend for one more night."

ALMA TRIED NOT TO BE NERVOUS AS THE TWO OF them walked across the street to the club.

She wasn't acting anymore around him, and he knew it.

She realized he never acted.

She remembered all his reactions the first day at the club and how his body responded to hers. He was attracted to her. He was torn the night before when he told her it was ending. He wanted to linger the same way she did.

Why couldn't he tell her the truth and let her figure out if it was worth it to continue?

"Have we met in the past?" she asked as they waited for the light.

He dropped her hand. "I know this doesn't make a lot of sense to you. This isn't about you or me."

"Big grand conspiracy. Got it." She'd heard that often in her life. Things were about her father or the firm. It was never for her. Will was clear he didn't care about her father, so she couldn't figure out what was happening.

"It's one more night. Then you go back to your normal life."

She laughed. That was funny. She appreciated this break from her normal life, craved it. Once this was over, she'd have to figure out what savings she needed to leave Denver. She could go full-time at the firm for a while if it meant leaving sooner.

But she already heard the voices of her family in her head.

You can't leave right after your father is elected mayor. That will reflect badly on him.

She wouldn't live her life like that anymore.

Life with Will would be different. She couldn't pay half his rent immediately if she left the firm but stayed in Denver. But she'd find a flexible work arrangement and make up the difference eventually. He lived close to the theater so commuting for rehearsal would be easy. It'd be hard, but if she had him, she'd have all the love and support she'd need.

He'd cook her dinner and massage her feet after a long day.

None of that would happen. She'd leave Denver for a variety of reasons, and Will would stay.

They settled into the VIP lounge like the previous nights. But they skipped the alcoholic drinks. She wanted to be as clear-headed as possible.

"I need to tell you something," she said.

"What?" His eyes narrowed behind his mask.

"My sisters called me today. I gave them a version of the story we're telling everyone here."

"I'm sorry," he said. "I didn't mean for this to affect your real life." She appreciated that he knew what she was telling him without having to spell it out.

"It's fine. I don't date much, so they aren't expecting this to go anywhere."

"But still, this was for me. It shouldn't touch the people you care about," he said. "You're amazing, Alma. You'll find some—"

"Don't." She couldn't hear that from him.

He held her close. "You're supposed to be enjoying my company."

"I am." She plastered on her performance smile.

He leaned in to kiss her temple. "Tell me what you're thinking."

She inhaled to strengthen her resolve. It was time to be honest. Or at least continue with the honesty she had developed in the last few hours. "I've enjoyed myself the last few days. It's bittersweet it's ending."

He kissed her ever so lightly on the lips. "Don't focus on the ending. Let's have fun tonight, and we can worry about the rest tomorrow."

She leaned into the kiss without deepening it, knowing she was ready to risk it all for him.

"Do you dance?" Will leaned into her ear and held the side of her face. The music was loud. That was why he needed to be close to her.

Sure.

"I can dance." Alma smiled.

His question was a formality. He knew what she was capable of. She wouldn't get far in her theater career if she couldn't dance.

"Let's dance." He stood up and offered her his hand. He couldn't get close enough to her in the lounge. They had a good time there. He loved that she charmed even his most famous or intimidating clients. But he was selfish with the time remaining.

On the dance floor, he'd lose himself in her body and ignore everything else.

"I'm not sure I'll be good at this kind of dancing."

"Don't worry. I'll lead. Stay with me."

She held his hand. He didn't think about how right this felt or how much she belonged in his life. They started this agreement pretending to be together, but they fell into a new space. They were together. No more pretending. But they both knew this expired in a few hours.

Will had imagined this weekend for years. Eros was his dream ever since he sneaked into clubs at seventeen with a fake ID. As he got older and recognizable as the son of the mayor, he thought of any way to be anonymous. Then he'd know his success was based on merit alone, and he didn't have to live up to anyone's idea of who he was.

He didn't merely want Eros; he wanted an empire. Clubs, bars, restaurants, everything. If people went out for a good night on the town, he wanted it to be at one of his establishments. It wasn't even wholly that he liked to party, which he did, but he liked to give it to other people.

He loved the delight on people's faces when they tasted an expertly mixed cocktail. Or Alma's when she took a bite of the pasta he made her.

As they entered the dance floor, he was almost glad for his mother's scheming. It meant he got to share this life event with Alma.

But he hated how Judy sought to bring an innocent woman down for a better chance of winning her election. It didn't even matter that the plan was doomed to fail because no one would care that Alma had fun. It didn't reflect badly on her or her father.

Not to mention the complete hypocrisy of the fact that he was the one who led her to these so-called bad decisions. His behavior would never cause a scandal.

But none of that mattered now as they moved together with the music. All he cared about was doing something he loved with this woman. He loved her body against his and how well she moved with him.

He knew she felt his arousal through his pants, but she didn't move away. She inched closer instead and when he heard her moan in his ear, he snapped.

He was going to fuck her on the dance floor or in the bathroom or in the lounge if he didn't do something quickly.

"I need to get a drink," he whisper-yelled to her.

She nodded. A flash of doubt formed across her face.

"You okay?" he asked when they got to the lounge.

"Yes." She shook her head. "I thought we were having fun and then you stopped."

Right. She didn't trust his feelings for her.

He kissed her, pouring everything he could into her. "We were having too much fun. I can't fuck you in front of five hundred of our closest friends."

"Was that a concern?"

"You were there with me. What do you think?"

She gave him a heated look. "Should we head to your apartment then?"

He wanted that. To take her home and strip her down and slide into her. He'd never desired another woman as much as he wanted Alma.

"That's not part of your job description."

"I didn't think I was working anymore."

"You're not." He looked away, wrestling with his craving for her and his need to protect her, even from himself.

If they did sleep together, he'd need to show his face, and she'd know he was using her.

It wasn't an option.

He'd do anything to be able to tell her the truth and still have her trust him. Soon. He'd give her whatever she needed to forgive him. He would grovel. It would take time. He might have to disown his family to do it, but he would sacrifice for her. He wouldn't sleep with her while he was still deceiving her.

Tonight, he'd keep her at the club until closing. She'd be too exhausted to do anything but sleep and then things could go according to his plan.

Easy.

"Let's stay," he said.

She nodded, and he'd give anything to tell her what he was thinking. But even if it was the time, it wasn't the place.

The lounge filled up, and partygoers crowded their table.

Alma plastered on her fake smile and invited everyone to join her in a drinking game.

WILL'S PLAN FELL APART. ALMA SAT ON HIS LAP AND his erection rubbed her ass. He touched the exposed skin on her back and restrained himself from whispering filthy things into her ear.

He needed her to know how he felt.

Until things could be different, his fantasy where the two of them were together and happy and in love lived a little longer.

The drinking games ended and most of the patrons drifted to the dance floor. It was late, but it was still at least an hour before last call.

"Let's get out of here." She stood and kept his hand in hers. He looked at her eyes that were partially hidden but were filled with trust and lust and he hoped something more.

He didn't protest. He couldn't deny her anything. All his good intentions for the night slipped away. As if, for her, the end of this night was inevitable.

She led him out of the club, moving deliberately and slowly. It could have been her heels or her tiredness or her arousal, but he was thankful for it.

It gave him more time until it all imploded.

"Let's grab cupcakes."

She stopped when he did, looking at the line that stretched out before them. He could have skipped it again and been the total asshole who put himself above everyone else, but he wasn't doing that again.

He had done it to put her above everyone else. She was important to him. Tonight, it was a delay tactic, a chance for a few more minutes with her before she discovered his betrayal.

She shook her head. "Let's go home."

Her heels echoed through the lobby and her lips crashed with his as soon as they entered the elevator.

He held her close to him, needing to consume her, forgetting to slow this down. He scattered kisses down her neck and pulled her knee to his hip, opening her up to him.

He brought his lip back to her mouth. She moaned as he deepened the kiss, but the elevator door opened too soon.

He let go of her leg and walked her backward until they got to his apartment door without breaking the rest of their connection. Her touch was essential to him. He pressed her against the wood as she kissed his exposed skin and undid the buttons of his shirt while he tried and failed to unlock the door.

Once inside, he flipped on the light, and to his surprise, she turned it off.

"No, I like the dark," she said.

As hot as that made him, he needed to slow this down. "Alma, wait. We need to talk about this."

"Will, it's fine. I know this isn't going anywhere. But I want tonight." She had his shirt open and was untucking it from his pants. Without thinking, he removed his jacket and tossed it onto the couch.

Fuck, his own body betrayed him.

"Alma, you won't go through with this if you know who I am."

She didn't stop. "Doesn't give you much incentive to tell me then."

He loved her. He needed to do this right. He grabbed her hands from his belt. "Please, let me tell you so you won't regret this."

Chapter Nine

Alma froze and looked at him. In the dark and beneath his mask, she searched his eyes for answers.

She didn't understand. Who the hell was he that she would regret sleeping with him?

"Do we know each other? Did I already reject you?"

"No, it's not about you or me."

She retreated. It was never about her. It was her father or the firm and soon it would be the city. Will said he didn't care about her father.

Panic seized her. "Will sleeping with me get you what you want?"

He stepped in close to her, breathing hard. His hands skimmed her neck until they reached the back of her head. His forehead rested on hers. "Sleeping with you was never the plan. But I want this. I want you. This. What happens in this apartment is about us."

She believed him. It wasn't time to consider what happened outside the apartment. "Are you trying to hurt me?"

"No, I would never."

She needed to decide. She could take the risk—let him tell

her who he is, make him explain everything. Why he needed her and no one else by his side this weekend.

It couldn't be as bad as he thought. Not if he wouldn't hurt her. Not when he'd protected her.

Or they could skip the truth and keep the masks between them. The truth couldn't hurt her if she didn't know it.

"I know you haven't told me everything, but have you lied to me?"

He kissed her forehead. She closed her eyes with the gesture. He'd done it over and over. It was what he did when he wanted more from her but couldn't press.

It was real affection from him.

"I sought you out. It's not an accident it's you here."

That wasn't an answer.

The puzzle pieces started to fall into place, but she swiped them away.

"But this is real? This is about us?"

"Yes."

Few things in her life had been about her. But this one thing could be. She could have a night with Will, and she'd walk away in the morning.

Her heart would ache, but maybe it would be better than whatever he withheld.

Everything couldn't be as terrible as he claimed. But she decided at the start of the weekend that she didn't need to know who he was. She trusted him.

She'd see this through.

In for a penny, in for a pound.

"I'm okay with this," Alma said finally.

Will drew her closer to him and held her tight. "I can't have you regretting this. You deserve so much more."

"I get to decide what I want and what I deserve. I want you. Whoever you are. Whatever you've done. I trust this."

She flattened her palm to the left side of his chest over his heart. His skin was smooth and his muscles firm, but underneath, she felt his heart racing.

They stayed still for a moment. Breathing in each other. Pausing in the heat. Letting their emotions simmer until they became something more. She was clear about what she meant. It was his turn to move.

He inched away from her. She couldn't see any details of his face, except his eyes. He stared into hers and then reached to untie her mask.

He then removed his own.

"One perfect night," he said. "And know that whatever happens, whatever comes of this, I care about you, and you are perfect." Whatever secrets he hid. Whatever dark forces were working against them, it didn't matter.

He carried her to the bedroom, kissing her the whole way. Their chemistry had been evident from their first meeting, but it morphed into something more. Now they finally allowed themselves to remove the walls holding them back.

He kissed with his whole body, his abs flexing as he carried her. His hips reached for hers. And his cock hardened like it knew it wouldn't be long until it was buried deep in her.

He eased her down onto the mattress and then removed his shirt, the shape of him visible in the shadows. She tried to sit up to worm out of her dress, but he stopped her with a kiss. "Let me do this. I need to do this," he whispered into her lips.

She nodded. Words became difficult. But he'd take care of her body.

He kissed his way down her front, pausing between her breasts where her dress had a deep V, but not touching either one. She squirmed and ran her hands through his hair, hoping to guide him where she wanted.

He chuckled and caressed her sides, again avoiding her breasts. "Patience, my soul. If I only get to do this once, I'm going to drag it out."

She suppressed a moan at the endearment. It was a translation of her name—it didn't have to mean anything. But she wanted to mean more to him than this one night.

Her heart raced at the thought he could be the end for her. If they got past whatever separated them and could be together.

She'd support him at the club.

He'd wait for her after performances.

It didn't need to be so difficult.

Will was determined to stay in the moment, and so she would, too.

He continued his trek down her body, kissing her everywhere, except the spots that had been forbidden to him. He paused at her belly button and her hip bones, and when she tried to open her legs for him, he gently closed them. She almost growled at him. Her panties were soaked, and she needed him to touch her. She'd never been so aroused or so adored.

He kissed the outside of her knees and then her ankles before he reached her feet.

He removed one shoe and then the other. "It was so fucking sexy seeing these on you all night. I'd imagined how good they'd make your ass look, but you always exceed my expectations."

"You could leave them on. Then they'd dig into your back while you fuck me."

His body covered hers in a second, and he kissed her again. "You're so needy, aren't you?" he said. She widened her hips to allow him to sink between them, forcing her dress to creep up her thighs. He was hard, and she shifted ever so slightly so her clit found the friction she craved.

"You're not giving me enough."

"Yet." He nibbled on her earlobe while his hand finally gripped her breast. "I love the idea of fucking you while you're wearing the clothes I bought you. I've thought about it all weekend. We get this once. I want nothing between us."

"Condom?" she asked, hoping for the exception.

"Of course. I take my responsibility to protect you seriously."

She squeezed her eyes shut. This was new territory for her. Every other man she had been with had been carefully vetted. They were someone her family approved of enough to introduce her to them, or she'd been with them long enough she truly believed they were in it for her. She'd been alone for so long. She hadn't known she needed *this* man.

He pushed the straps of her dress down her shoulders and tugged at the neckline to expose her nipples to the air. He couldn't see her, but she felt revealed.

She reached between them to undo his belt, then undid the button and inched the zipper down. He moaned as she brushed his cock. She expected him to stop her again and tell her she was going too fast, but he let her.

His mouth was on her nipple, kissing and sucking. Each touch was meant to draw pleasure from her.

His pants were open, but she couldn't touch him the way she wanted with how her straps were positioned. She pushed on his shoulder so she could maneuver out of her dress.

"I need your skin against mine," she said when he hesitated to separate their bodies.

He moved them both to their knees but continued to hold her against his chest. "Hold onto me." Will slowly peeled the dress down her body, each inch of skin exposed immediately pressed to his. Like he was trying to memorize the feel of her.

While she clung to him, he removed his pants. They collapsed onto the bed, and she giggled, taking her time to outline the muscles in his arms and on his back, wanting to feel all of him.

He read her mind and braced himself in a pushup position

for her perusal. She sketched the smooth skin of his chest, feeling his muscles and the slight layer of sweat that had accumulated.

She didn't want to tell him what she was thinking. That she wanted to see him. That she wanted to memorize the lines of his abs. That there was no truth he could tell her in this moment that would stop her from following through with her choices.

But he had been so sure.

"Flip onto your back," she ordered.

She saw his head tilt to the side in confusion.

"Why?"

"Because I want to kiss your abs and then suck your cock." She wasn't usually this explicit in bed, but with Will, it was easy to say exactly what she wanted.

"No."

"Okay." That hurt.

"Alma, babe. If my cock gets anywhere near your mouth right now, I'm going to come embarrassingly fast. Let me make you feel good, and then we can talk about all the wet places you'll take me."

She wasn't in this alone.

He sat on his heels and placed his hands on her hips, using one finger to dip under the elastic on her panties.

"I wondered if you thought it was inappropriate that I picked out your underwear. I told myself it was because it needed to work with the dresses."

"I'm an actor. I'm used to working with costumes that dictate every stitch of fabric I wear," she said.

"That's what I'd hoped. But I imagined taking it off you," he said and then dragged her thong down her legs.

She was finally naked in front of him and while she could see the shadow of him and that was all he could see of her, it still felt like he examined every piece of her.

She wondered if she held up to his scrutiny.

He skimmed his hands up the inside of each leg and when he reached the top, he applied the slightest pressure. She complied with his request and opened her legs for him.

"Tell me to stop, and I'll stop," he said.

"I don't want you to stop," she said.

He kissed her mouth one more time before he settled his face between her legs.

They moaned together as his tongue flattened against her opening. She was already so wet for him she didn't need him to prepare her any more. He had to be aware of that. This was to make her feel good.

He sucked on her clit and tested her, plunging one finger inside. Her back arched off the bed and she lifted her hips to get closer to him. He responded by pumping into her harder and using his other hand to hold her hip down. His tongue flicked and caressed, testing different pressures and movements until she gasped.

"Fuck, just like that."

She felt him grin against her mound.

She loved his smile. She loved how he did it for only her.

The feelings she had for him were making the sensation more intense. He added a second finger, and it wouldn't be long before she crashed through an orgasm that would shatter her mind, body, and soul.

She drew her hands through his hair, needing to be closer to him in any way possible. Without being able to see anything, she focused on what she felt. The movements of his tongue. The spread of his fingers. The scrape of his scruff on her thigh.

"Will, I'm so close," she panted.

"Yes, Alma. Come for me."

Her hand found his on her hip, and he squeezed her fingers. It felt like a promise. The small act of affection sent her over the edge into an orgasm so intense she felt like she left her body.

He continued to lick and suck as the waves of pleasure washed through her.

As her breathing slowed, he removed his hand and gently kissed her thigh. "Good girl. That was amazing."

She smiled. She hadn't regained her ability to speak, but she noticed something odd in his voice. She wondered if it was regret.

"Yes," she said finally. She had to tell him she was okay and wanted more from him.

She pulled on his hand, so he'd come closer. Their mouths found each other in the dark, and she held him to her as if to tell him what they shared already wasn't nearly enough.

"I want you," she said.

"Are you sure? It's not too late to change your mind about any of this. We can stop."

"I don't want to stop. I know what I want and, Will, I know you. You'll always take care of me." She paused. This was her last chance to confirm she was right about him. She knew his soul the same as he knew hers. "Unless I'm wrong."

He held her face in his hands. Her legs wrapped around his waist. The hard length of his cock rubbed her through the cloth of his boxers.

"You're not wrong," he breathed into her ear. "I'd do anything for you."

"I'll still leave in the morning and never know all the ways you could hurt me."

"I wish this could be different."

"Me too," she said. "But this will be enough."

She heard fabric rustling as he found his wallet in his pants.

He kissed her briefly and then removed his boxers and rolled the condom on. He positioned himself at her entrance and then braced one arm next to her head. She brushed her fingers down his back until she got to his hips.

He entered her slowly, fulfilling his promise to take his time with her. Each inch of him stretched her out as she lifted her hips to meet his. She groaned when he was finally buried to the hilt, his pelvic bone hit her already sensitive clit. She'd never been so full or so close to anyone.

"Fuck, you're so tight." He moved slowly in her, pulling out part way and then rolling his hips, making her feel him everywhere. Like with his kisses, he did this with his whole body. His back muscles rippled beneath her hands. His thighs spread her wide, and his hands cradled her head. Her body and soul were completely consumed by him.

She lost herself. This moment was the most vibrant of her life. Every sensation in her body was amplified, and all her emotions threatened to explode out of her body.

He was slow and methodical. Like he had every move coordinated in advance for maximum bliss. He thrust in and out of her, hitting the right angle to brush against her clit.

She rushed toward a second orgasm, something she rarely experienced, but she wasn't ready for this to be over.

"Wait, wait, wait."

Will's head was buried in her neck, but he pushed back up. "What's wrong?"

"Nothing. I'm getting close."

"That's the point, darling." He kissed the corners of her mouth.

"I want more."

He lazily rolled his hips. "I can give you more."

Her breath caught. She wanted everything from him. There would be time for those thoughts later. Now, the only important thing was how he filled her, hitting just the right spots to make her see stars.

This whole weekend, he'd been in control. He'd been the

one to make decisions for them. She loved that she trusted him so much and he hadn't let her down. Not once.

But she wanted him to trust her with their pleasure.

"Flip onto your back, please?" God, she wanted to see his face to know what he was thinking.

He held her tight and rolled them both. She giggled when they got dangerously close to falling off the edge of the bed, their chests pressed against each other.

"Happy?" Will asked.

"Ecstatic." She shifted to move upright with the intent to ride him.

"No." His voice panicked, and he grasped her upper arms. "I need you close. Don't take that away from me." She relaxed down and folded over him, so he could wrap his arms around her. "Not yet."

She fell into his movement, matching his every thrust. She was cherished, protected, and worshipped.

He held her tight, and she took him in deep as they tried to occupy the same space.

Her orgasm rushed toward her, never having felt so open or secure in her connection with her partner. She came hard, her walls collapsing around him as he stroked her back and whispered in her ear. Her brain short-circuited and she shook around him, waves seeming to go on and on.

"Fuck, that felt amazing," Will said. He held her by the nape of the neck as he bucked up into her one last time. "Alma!"

He stilled at the end of his release, and she remained unable to move.

He rolled her onto her back and pulled out of her. But she couldn't process any of that as she tried to figure out what he had whispered while she was coming. She'd heard him say "love," but she had no idea if the word "I" was immediately before or "you" immediately after because they were all jumbled together, and her brain couldn't put anything in order.

She reached for him and heard his chuckle.

"I'll be right back, Alma."

A moment later, he returned to the space next to her. His hand drifted over her cheek, and he gently turned her head to look at him.

He was on his side facing her.

Slowly, she turned onto her side.

They were nose to nose, his hand resting on her cheek while she traced the lines of his face with her fingers.

"What happens in the morning now?" she asked. Everything had changed. There was no going back from what they had done.

"I'll wake up before you. Make you breakfast. And then I'll leave." He kissed her fingertips. "If at any point you change your mind about knowing who I am, you know where to find me."

"But you don't want that." She moved her hand close to her chest as if it could protect her heart.

He didn't speak right away. And when he did, he spoke slowly. "I want you to be happy. I don't want to hurt you."

"This is hurting me anyway."

"It's hurting me, too," Will said.

"Knowing the truth will hurt?"

"I don't want it to, but it will."

"Is it a hurt we can get over?"

"I don't know."

She sat with his words. She trusted him even while he told her not to. She believed he cared about her. No one could make love that passionately without feeling something for their partner.

People might fake it all the time, but that wasn't this.

He kissed her gently, and it tasted like goodbye. "You'll always know where to find me, Alma. I promise."

She held in her tears. She didn't point out to him that he was the one who found her. He knew her full name when she didn't know his. But she accepted his promise.

She rolled to her other side and he wrapped an arm around her stomach. She was exhausted and drained and never wanted to leave his bed and his arms.

Chapter Ten

Will fought his need to sleep. He got one night with Alma and couldn't lose any of it.

They had been so perfect together. Each time he found something that brought her pleasure it rocketed right back to him. He'd held off his orgasm as long as possible, needing to know what it felt like for her to come on his cock.

It had been beyond heavenly.

A catastrophic experience that changed him forever.

He was Alma's for the rest of his life. It didn't matter what happened in the morning or in the upcoming weeks, she ruined him for anyone else.

But it didn't change what he needed to do. He'd sneak out of the bedroom, hating that they wouldn't be able to make love in the morning sunlight. He'd cook her breakfast and leave. He'd go to his other apartment and figure out how to keep Club Eros open without his mother's funding.

The rock star expressed interest in investing. There had to be others who wanted in.

Just because it was the end of things with Alma didn't

mean it had to be the end of all his dreams. Just the one where he was in love and happy.

Maybe it wouldn't be so bad if Alma walked in on him in the kitchen tomorrow. She might see things differently than he did. After everything he told her the night before, she had to suspect. Not all the details, but enough to maybe not be surprised by the truth.

He hadn't lied to her. She knew he targeted her for her family. She didn't know why, but it was enough.

He loved her. He knew that for certain. He'd walk to the underworld itself if it meant he could be with her.

He held her close to his chest as her breathing slowed, and she fell into sleep.

IT TOOK A FEW MOMENTS FOR ALMA TO CENTER herself when she woke up. The sheets were soft against her bare skin, and the light was much brighter than her room at home.

Her entire body was pleasurably sore, and she was not alone. She faced away from Will to open her eyes. She didn't know the time. Her purse with her phone had been discarded in the living room. The room had an alarm clock, but it was on the nightstand on Will's side of the bed.

She was so close to breaking the rules. After three days of not being able to see him, knowing he was next to her and vulnerable made her feel weird. Like she broke his trust.

Everything changed. He said if she ever changed her mind about knowing the truth, she knew where to find him. He was willing to tell her everything. She was the one who wanted to live in the fantasy where nothing hurt her and she was the center of someone's world.

She wasn't. She wasn't even the center of Will's world.

He had all but confirmed whatever reason they were brought together had to do with her family or the law firm when he'd said it wasn't an accident he'd reached out to her. She hadn't wanted the truth last night. She was too caught up in the moment to care.

It was worth it. Their connection was too passionate and strong to be anything other than genuine.

Whatever was going on with him, they'd get through it together. They'd tested their foundation and found it strong. She'd had the best sex of her life with him. No matter what happened next, she had that. But she wanted more from him. She wasn't entirely sure what the future had in store for her, but she wanted to try for something with Will. She cared about him too much to let him go without a fight.

To do that, she needed to see his face.

She should close her eyes and nudge him awake. He'd make her breakfast and then leave. She'd spend a few days weighing her options. That might be easier. She'd text him and talk with him on the phone, tell him how she felt and know for sure he felt the same.

He could tell her the truth then.

They could make this decision together.

But she might lose her nerve, and he was right next to her.

Whatever it was, it wouldn't be a big deal. They'd get over it fast, and he could be inside her again in a matter of minutes. She was already hot imagining looking into his eyes while they had sex.

She rolled onto her other side and sat up, bringing the sheet with her to cover her breasts. She didn't need the first thing he saw to be her nakedness. Not when they needed to have a serious conversation.

Her gaze fell on his chest first. She eyed the muscles she'd stroked the night before. He rested on his back with one hand relaxed on his stomach. The sheet artfully covered him from the waist down.

The lines of his muscles were well-defined; he had to spend hours at the gym. No one looked like that without massive intervention and a genetic predisposition.

Her gaze then tracked his exposed skin up to his face. His eyes were still closed, and so she took her time looking at him, memorizing the man she'd spent the last three days with. The man who had been inside her a few hours before.

He took her breath away.

She'd known he was gorgeous. A mask only covers so much. But seeing his face all together without interruption was like looking at the sunrise. Beautiful and overwhelming.

A faint sense of familiarity trickled in the back of her mind. A pre-teen she knew who eventually became a man she saw occasionally from a distance.

William Caron.

Why did the mayor's son want her?

Not her. Her father.

"Oh fuck."

His eyes shot open as she tried to retreat from him. She practically fell out of bed, dragging the sheet with her.

"Alma, wait."

She backed up against the wall, making sure she was covered. "What did you do?"

"Nothing, I swear." He got out of bed, and she closed her eyes. She didn't want to see him naked.

She spent so much of her life with people wanting things from her—a job at the family firm, a lawyer to get them money after a dispute, connections to wealth.

She had forgotten about the new aspect of her life.

Politics.

If the Carons were involved, it wasn't because they wanted something from her. It was because she was in their way.

All the puzzle pieces she ignored the night before suddenly fell into place.

"The blog article about my costumes, that was you?"

She heard fabric rustling and opened her eyes to see he'd put on pants.

"It wasn't me."

"But it was your mother."

"She pushed me into a corner. Please, Alma. Let's get dressed. I'll make coffee and breakfast, and I'll explain everything to you."

"I don't want to hear any more lies!"

"I'm not lying to you." He sounded frustrated, like he was trying not to raise his voice.

A thousand terrible scenarios ran through her head as she watched him pace the room from her spot on the floor. Did she do anything dumb on Thursday night when she was drunk? Were her dresses short enough that someone could have gotten an upskirt picture?

Had he filmed them in bed the night before?

She thought she might vomit. She trusted him. She trusted her gut that he cared about her when it was clearly all a lie to win a stupid election.

He crossed to her side of the bed.

"Stay away from me."

He froze where he was. "Okay. I'll be right here. This is what it looks like. But I never intended to go through with it. Judy is losing, and she tried to compromise you to taint your father. She is my main investor, and she threatened to cut my funding if I didn't carry out her plan."

"Oh my god. You'd really hurt someone to keep your precious club open?" She couldn't imagine purposefully damaging another person for personal gain.

"No, of course not. I was stalling. I saw you in *Midsummer*, and I thought I could go through the motions.

Tell her that I took you to the club and even with my best efforts I couldn't get you to misbehave. I tried to talk her out of it, but she wouldn't listen."

"I can't hear this right now." She didn't know what was the truth and what was a lie anymore. She had been so sure of how he felt, but this was a new game for her. She didn't know the rules when someone sabotaged you for their own gain. "Please leave."

"I'll go. Take as much time as you need. I'll call you later, and we can talk about this."

She looked around at the blank room. She should have seen it. There were so many signs she ignored. "Is this even your apartment?"

"Yes. Sort of. I got it for nights when I'm at the club late. I live in another place a few miles from here."

"How can I ever trust you?" Her voice broke. It wasn't only the past few days, but the future together she'd begun to imagine for them.

He shook his head and moved to the closet, knowing better than to remind her that he told her not to. "Trash the place if you want. I won't blame you. You deserve so much better than this."

When he emerged, he wore jeans and a long-sleeved Henley. She remained rooted to the ground. "You don't have to pick up my call. I'll leave you a voicemail explaining everything. You can go to the press if that'll help."

"You think that's what I want? My life and my choices torn apart in the media because of my relationship to men?"

"It doesn't matter what I think. I want to give you what you need to make your own choices. And we both know she can't win. Not after this."

She clenched her jaw. "You'd go against your own mother?"

He didn't hesitate. "For you? Yes. Easy."

"Will." Her voice was barely above a whisper.

"I swear to you, Alma. Last night was real. That was us. You may never forgive me, but I will always stand by you and support you, no matter what."

She was too stunned to respond, so he left the bedroom and a moment later, she heard the front door close.

WILL STORMED OUT OF HIS APARTMENT, BARELY able to function, and only got dressed properly because of his mental checklist.

Keys.

Wallet.

Sunglasses.

Shoes.

He shoved everything into the pockets of his coat as he left. Focusing on what he needed to do kept him from freezing in panic.

He spent the drive to his parents' rehearsing his speech. His mother might decide to come clean, but no matter what, he'd make it clear he was no longer on her side. He'd burn down his relationship with his family.

It was past time. Then he would put Alma first. He meant it when he said he'd leave a message outlining everything. She could take it to the press; he didn't care. He wanted her back, and he wanted her forgiveness, and he wanted her in his bed. But more than that, he wanted her strong and powerful and to have all the information to do what was best for her.

He thought he was best for her. He could be what was best for her. But he'd accept her anger first and do anything to earn her trust again.

He'd even prepare for the chance she wouldn't. But that outcome was better than letting his mother get away with what she'd done. He didn't care how many trials he went through for that to happen.

He loved Alma. He'd been falling since the first moment he saw her on stage. She was worth whatever wrath he brought down on himself.

The house was quiet when he arrived. The household staff were discreet, and his parents were at church. It was a ritual more to do with being seen than any actual devotion. In the hierarchy of his mother's hypocrisy, this one didn't bother him too much. Usually, she used it as an opportunity to talk to constituents and connect with her community, and so at least some good came out of it.

She used to care about issues and had projects to better the city. Sometime in the last few years, she'd changed and only cared about staying in power.

All the villainous tendencies he remembered from his youth started to trickle into her campaign.

In the kitchen, he helped himself to a cup of coffee and toast. He'd planned to make Alma eggs benedict. He hoped she got something to eat before she went home. He kind of hoped she trashed the apartment. That was appropriate. She deserved so much better than him.

But he'd fight to be good enough for her.

Maybe he'd get another chance to wake her up to the smell of ham cooking.

The front door opened and his parents came into the kitchen. His dad wore a light gray suit, and his mother a plum dress.

While his shirt and jeans were clean, his body wasn't. He hadn't showered since he spent hours dancing, and his skin was covered in both his and Alma's sweat.

But he'd never been more determined or in control.

"Will, I wasn't expecting you this early," Judy said. "I assume you have something for me."

He leaned against the counter as she poured herself a cup of coffee.

"No, I have nothing for you." He couldn't hide the venom in his voice and didn't intend to.

"I'm disappointed you chased my guests out of the club the other day. But I'm sure you had your reasons."

"Eros has a strict code of conduct. Drug usage results in immediate removal and lifetime bans. They pulled it out right in front of one of my security guards."

He didn't know why he argued with her about this. It didn't matter. Alma should never have been put in any danger in the first place.

"I'm sure you tried your best. You can't lose your funding. You love that club. I hear the opening numbers were higher than expected."

He didn't care about Eros anymore. He'd find another investor, but even if he lost the club, it wouldn't be as bad as losing Alma. He'd spent years working in the nightclub and entertainment industry. He'd figure out how to continue.

"I came here to tell you Alma knows everything. Or almost everything. And whatever she doesn't know now, I'll tell her."

His mother sipped her coffee. "I'll deny everything. And you won't tell. This scandal will bring you down, too."

"I don't care if I go down as long as you go down with me. I told you from the beginning Alma didn't deserve this. It'll be up to her what she does with it. But she'll have my full support."

"You won't betray me like this for some girl."

"She's not some girl. I love her. You might have been a good mayor once, but I'll do everything I can to keep you from being re-elected. I'll endorse Charles Blake, and how will that look for you?"

A look crossed her face he couldn't read. Was it possible

she was bluffing? Considering the consequences of her actions? "Say goodbye to your club, your apartments, and the rest of your lifestyle."

"I don't know why you think I care about that anymore. This isn't about that. I'm done with you. I'm sure you will care more about losing your position and your power than you do about losing your son."

He stormed out of the house and was at his car when he realized his father followed him.

"Will, wait!" Robert had been there the whole time and hadn't said a word. He was just as guilty in this as his mother as far as Will was concerned. "I know you are going to tell Alma everything, but we need a strategy for damage control."

"Damage control? What are you talking about? I'm trying to do damage."

"You're not concerned that Alma talking to the press will hurt you?"

"I don't care if it hurts me. She trusted me, and I betrayed her. I'll take the consequences." Alma wouldn't throw him under the bus. He thought he knew her well. She was far too trusting, and she'd give him the chance to explain. They might not have a relationship the way he wanted, but that was a price he would pay if she was okay.

"Don't do anything rash."

"Look, this is your chance. If you want to stand by this nonsense, fine. I'm done with you, too."

"Don't do this, Will. We love you."

"I'm sure you do. You love power more."

"I'm trying to protect you."

"No, you're protecting her."

"It might not look like it, but she's doing all of this for you —to make the world better for you."

"You can do that without hurting me or anyone else."

He got into his car, his father not bothering to say anything else.

He checked the time as he drove out of their neighborhood. Alma should be home by now. He used his phone's voice command to call her and, after the first ring, everything went black.

Chapter Eleven

THE NOISE OF THE CAMPAIGN OFFICE THREATENED to overwhelm Alma as she walked in early Sunday afternoon. The room bustled with activity. Volunteers sought quiet corners to make calls. Staff trained people on scripts for canvassing. Most wore green "Blake for Mayor" T-shirts and looked pleased and determined to get the word out about Denver's most famous citizen.

A few people stopped her as she walked to the rear office. She expected that. She couldn't walk into a room with her family name on the door and her face exposed and not expect to be recognized.

She ached for the masks she wore all weekend.

A pang of understanding spread through her. Will experienced this. It was a genius idea to create a new world where no one knew his identity.

She smiled at a field organizer to stop herself from crying. They could have shared this. He didn't need to deceive and lie to her. He could have reached out, and everything would have been fine.

After she got home from Will's, Alma spent far too long in

the shower, first trying to wash her body of all the evidence of Will, then remembering everything he had said. It mattered to him. He cared about her. He would destroy his relationship with his mother for her. It had been the best sex of her life, and she'd fallen asleep believing she was in love with him.

She covered the worst evidence of her crying with makeup and dressed in jeans with a cable knit sweater. She wanted to hide in her clothes and leave nothing for commentary.

She was done living in other people's expectations. Her father's. Will's.

But a part of her heard Will cheering her on.

She wasn't entirely sure where things stood with them, if a future between them was on the table. After she calmed down a bit and repeated their conversation, she'd appreciated he hadn't dug in deeper. He didn't tell her she was crazy or try to deny it. She didn't fully understand his involvement, but it was clear he didn't think they were over.

For you? Yes. Easy.

Alma had a strained relationship with her dad at the moment, but it would get better. She sure as hell wouldn't tank his career on a whim.

Will had yet to follow through on his promise to tell her everything with a voicemail to take to the press. He'd called while she showered but didn't leave a message.

But, as he told her last night, this wasn't about them.

Alma found her father with his campaign manager, Grady, in the small office that stored yard signs and T-shirts. It was a step down from the corner office he occupied at Blake Smith, but campaigns were about images more than they were about ideas.

The image of Charles Blake spreading out to ask donors for money while the rest of his staff sat on the floor was a bad one.

Charles Blake, elbow to elbow with volunteers and

economical with his spending, showed he'd be a good custodian of the city's finances once he got the job.

Everything was about appearances.

"Alma, I didn't expect you until later," he said after she knocked on the door.

"I know. I need to talk with you," she said.

"This isn't a good time. Grady and I are in the middle of something." He pointed to his computer monitor. Grady gave her a look indicating he questioned her audacity to ask for time with her father.

She never liked the man. He focused on the end goal of getting her father elected and didn't care who he stepped on. He only cared about Charles Blake because he thought it could be a chance at the next big job.

He'd probably get along well with Judy Caron.

"It's important. It's about Will Caron." She closed the door, barely muffling the noise behind it.

"I didn't know you knew him," Charles said.

"I didn't. But he was the man I was with all weekend."

"Stop talking. Grady, get out." He stood, entering full lawyer mode.

"What?" Grady said.

"Alma signed an NDA. You need to leave," Charles said.

"Given what I said, do you think the NDA is a concern right now?" Alma said. If Will followed through and told her everything, the NDA wouldn't matter anymore. He'd release her from it.

The man she was with last night would never enforce it. It was probably something his mother required him to do in the first place. Alma knew the real version of Will.

Grady looked to Charles who nodded and then left the office.

"They can fuck around all they want. I won't do anything they can attack me for," Charles said.

Alma bit into the inside of her lip until she tasted blood. "It doesn't concern you that he went to all that effort to hide who he was from me?"

"Of course, that concerns me. But I told you not to go through with it. I told you the job was a bad idea. If this hurts the campaign..."

"It won't. I didn't do anything to embarrass you or the campaign. Your shiny reputation is fine. But what about me? Did you think of your image and your campaign before you thought of me and my safety?"

"You're standing in front of me. Clearly you're fine. I care, but that doesn't change that you put yourself in that position."

Alma fumed. This wasn't her fault. And even Will wouldn't tell her it was. He was the liar. He held the blame. Not her.

Her dad held his ambition above everything else. He alone could make things better. He alone could build the legal practice he wanted.

There wasn't even a Smith. It was a name he added to his so people thought he had a partner when he started out. But all along it was only him.

Alma took a deep breath. She had performed in front of thousands of people. She could stand up to her father.

"Will is going to call me and explain what happened. I'll listen to him." She hadn't been sure of the next part until she saw her father's reaction. "Then I'm putting in my two weeks' notice at Blake Smith and looking at apartments." Will had already paid her. She could probably sell the dresses and shoes. She didn't want to dip into her savings until she left Denver, but she needed out of her parent's place more than she needed out of town.

"Excuse me?"

She was exhausted.

"Now you start listening? Because you haven't been listening when I said I don't want to go to law school, or now when I'm trying to tell you about what happened between Will and me. I know I've been coasting by working at the firm, but I won't do that anymore." Will had a lot to answer for, but she remembered the look he gave her in the hallway when he said he didn't care about her father or his own reputation.

That man expected her to stand up for herself. If he wasn't real, it didn't matter. He still saw the best version of her.

Charles sat down, processing her declaration.

"Okay. I'm listening now. What do I need to know about William?"

Alma gathered her thoughts for a moment and then continued. She told him about the makeup she wore and how Will had been so deliberate in the conversations they had about ground rules. She told him all the relevant details about the three nights she spent with him. How he'd been protective of her and took care of her. How she was certain he only wanted to spend time with her the night before.

She tried to filter out the physical things that transpired between them, but having logged thousands of depositions, her father knew when someone was hiding something.

He stared at his desk, rubbing his jaw. "Do you regret it?"

Alma paused. The answer came to her too fast. She needed to sit with it, so she knew it was real.

"No. I still trust him. He has a world of answering to do. I might not have figured out the details of the lies he told me, but I knew the truth when I heard it." *Or rather felt it.*

"You'd be a great lawyer. You're certainly making a case for him."

She smiled. For the first time in a long time, he heard what she was saying. "If I'm wrong, we'll deal with it."

"He means something to you? Even though you didn't know who he was?"

"I can't explain it."

"I met Will a few times. He's a good kid."

Alma rolled her eyes. "He's my age."

"You're a good kid, too."

"Thanks, Dad. What do we do now?"

"I guess we wait for his call. You heading home?"

"No, I'll hang out here for a bit. Do some 'get out the vote' calls. I can't let her win," she said.

ALMA SPENT MOST OF HER AFTERNOON LISTENING TO the ringing of people's phones. Few people answer the phone for an unknown number, and a lot of phones automatically silence unknown calls. But occasionally, someone picked up, and she reminded them that the mayoral election was coming up and encouraged them to vote for Charles Blake. She highlighted his accomplishments and his agenda for the city.

If someone asked about a comparison to Mayor Caron, she followed her script, even if her anger flared.

Her father tried to run a positive campaign as much as possible, especially since this was a nonpartisan race. No one ran on their party affiliation even if it was public knowledge where everyone stood. They were all Democrats; they all had similar values. Charles couldn't risk isolating anyone who might support him in the future.

Judy clearly didn't feel the same.

Alma was exhausted. Her body was still sore, and her throat had gone dry from talking. A few volunteers stopped by to speculate with her about how she thought they were doing. Others came by to ask about her auditions and if she tried for television or movies or Broadway.

She definitely didn't tell anyone about her latest job.

Her sisters pestered her for details about her weekend

when they grabbed flyers. She smiled and told them they would get drinks soon.

After a few hours, Alma was clarifying the vote-by-mail process to an elderly woman who couldn't leave her house easily when several phones went off at once, including hers. Alma focused on alleviating the woman's concerns but was aware the room went silent for a few seconds. Everyone read the same news notification.

Then multiple people swore, and the room erupted in conversation.

Alma finished her call and looked at her phone to see what the commotion was about.

The push notification was from a local news station.

"Denver mayor's son hospitalized after car accident; City Hall confirms."

The room started to spin.

Surely Will had a brother. Judy had another son, right?

But none of that was true.

"Alma!" her father called.

She looked up as he waved her to his office.

She sat down in a daze while Grady rushed in.

"I just got off the phone with Caron's campaign manager," Grady said. "Someone ran a stop sign and hit him. He's in surgery, but they don't know anything more."

"But he'll be okay?" Alma choked out.

"That's all she knows." Grady almost shrugged.

She looked at her phone, resisting the urge to call Will. It wouldn't matter since he was in surgery, but she thought maybe this was some weird joke, and if she called him, he'd pick up and tell her everything was okay. Someone made a mistake.

"Call everyone out of the field," Charles said.

"What?" Grady said.

"Shut everything down. I'm not campaigning while her son is on the operating table."

Alma looked at her father and understood what he was thinking, how he'd feel if the positions were reversed. If it had been Alma hurt while Judy knocked on doors and made phone calls and asked people for their votes and their money.

It was more than that, too. Voters might turn away if they thought he was callous and didn't put family first.

"Fine. You'll put out a statement. I'll send Hannah in." Grady left the room.

"He'll be fine," Charles said.

Alma smiled weakly at him. "You don't know that."

He opened his mouth to say something, but his communications director, Hannah, entered the room.

"I've already begun drafting," she said. "Standard language: 'We wish William a speedy recovery. Thoughts and prayers are with him and his family.'"

Alma flinched at the use of his full name. He was just Will to her.

"Anything to add?" Charles asked her.

"No, I just want to see him," Alma said.

Hannah looked confused.

"That'll have to wait. You can't go to the hospital. Not when you don't know what you're walking into."

Alma hated that.

"Someone will drive you home," Charles said. "I'll let you know as soon as I hear anything."

Alma didn't remember much about the drive home. She sat in the passenger seat of her own car while a volunteer tried to make small talk. No one asked her why she was so upset about the mayor's son's car accident.

At home, Alma poured herself a glass of wine, the chardonnay reminding her of Will. There wasn't anything for her to do, so she sat on the couch and turned on reality TV.

It wasn't too long before both her sisters showed up, still in their campaign shirts and holding their clipboards.

"Dad told us to check on you," Rachel said. Her eyes tracked the TV and the nearly empty bottle of wine.

She paused. "The boyfriend, the one with the nightclub, was Will Caron."

"Oh, sweetheart." Kayla sat down on the couch next to her. "Have you heard anything?"

She shook her head. "No. The whole thing was complicated."

"Wait, you used past tense. Did you break up?" Kayla asked.

"We had a fight. I don't know."

She'd talked herself in circles. She needed Will to be okay, even if things didn't work out between them. She couldn't stop blaming herself. She was the reason he was on the road. If she hadn't kicked him out of the apartment, he wouldn't have gotten into the car accident.

But she didn't have answers yet, so she sat with her sisters on the couch drinking wine.

It was her parents who forced her to eat something besides ice cream when they got home.

"I have a call from the mayor coming in," Charles announced.

Alma sat up taller as he moved closer to her.

He put the call on speaker.

"Mayor Caron, how are you?"

"Fuck, Charles, it's been a shitty day."

Alma had forgotten the two of them worked together in

the past. They had been friends. She wondered what happened to turn everything so toxic.

Or if it was inevitable.

"You are on speaker with my wife and daughters," he said.

Judy didn't speak for a moment.

"All your daughters?" she asked.

Charles held Alma's gaze. "Yes."

It took a moment for Alma to realize the sound coming out of the phone was crying. "I fucked up. I'm so sorry."

"Judy, we'll discuss that later." Her father held onto his leverage for when he needed it.

"I almost lost him, and it was so stupid of me."

Alma sucked in a breath. What exactly did she mean?

"How is he?" Charles asked.

Judy composed herself. "They put some pins in his leg, and he has a concussion. They're keeping him overnight."

"But he'll be okay?" Alma asked.

"Yes. I should go. Visiting hours are ending soon, and I want to be with him."

"I'm here if you need anything, Judy."

"Thanks, Charles. I know you won't let me off the hook for this."

"We're both ambitious. I'm sure we can come up with some solution."

As much of a relief as the news was, it didn't give Alma the closure she'd hoped for. It left her with more questions that wouldn't have answers until she spoke with Will.

And she didn't like her dad threatening the mayor.

Chapter Twelve

When Will woke after his leg surgery, his first thought was Alma. He didn't register his pain, only the need to be close to her and explain everything.

But then the crash came back to him.

His mother and father had been sitting by his bedside. He told them he'd speak with them concerning his medical issues, nothing else. He hadn't ever set boundaries with them until now. His mother tried to bring up the election, but he cut her off.

He had to stay in the hospital overnight and was preparing for the fight to send his parents home when his mother stepped out for a moment.

When she returned, her eyes were red. "I know you don't want to talk about anything beyond what we have to, but I thought you should know—I talked with Charles Blake."

Will didn't respond, so she continued.

"Alma was on the line. So she knows about your accident. She sounded concerned." Will felt nauseous. He needed to reach out to her. She was waiting for his explanation. He hated that she was spending all this time thinking the worst of him.

"Charles and I will talk in the next few days about the future of the campaign." She looked a little fearful.

Will wondered if they would come to some sort of arrangement without involving the press. Alma would have told her father what happened. He might have enough leverage to force Judy out of the race.

"I almost lost you, Will, and the last thing we would have talked about was me throwing you away..."

"I don't want to hear this right now," Will said. He didn't know if she had a change of heart or if this was another act. Others were forcing her to face the consequences of her actions. She never surrendered without someone else pulling the strings.

"I understand." She squeezed his hand and retreated to the chair where she kept her vigil.

Someone had retrieved Will's phone from the wreckage of his car and returned it to him. The doctor told him not to spend too much time looking at the screen because it would aggravate his concussion symptoms. He itched to text Alma and apologize, but any text he drafted would be too much and not nearly enough.

When his parents were finally kicked out by hospital staff, he called Alma.

"Will." She sounded breathless. It was late at night, and he hoped he hadn't woken her.

"Alma, babe." He was high on painkillers. This was probably a bad idea, but he needed to hear her voice. "I'm so sorry."

"I don't care about that right now. How are you?"

"I'll be fine." He needed to see her, but he didn't have any right to ask her to visit him. Especially not when his mother hovered so much. "I'll be out in a few days. Can I see you then?"

"Yes." She was crying.

"Alma, what's wrong?"

"I was scared. Scared you were going to die, and I would never know…"

"You know." He hated himself for hurting her, for giving her cause to cry. He loved her but wondered if it was enough to heal all the lies he told her.

He let her cry on the other end of the phone, knowing there was nothing for him to do now to ease her pain. Each tear was torture for him, and he felt like he earned all the pain he got. He'd spend the rest of his life making it up to her.

ALMA ADJUSTED THE HEM ON HER WRAP DRESS AS she stood outside the mayor's house. Will had texted her to tell her he was out of the hospital and staying at his parents' place. He wanted to talk.

She spent extra time on her appearance. She played other people so often that she didn't know how to dress herself sometimes. For all her speculation on the topic, she didn't know what kind of woman Will was attracted to. He'd dressed her stylishly at the club, so maybe that was it. But she wanted him to like her for who she was and not who she'd pretended to be.

She settled on a floral print dress, tights, and black boots.

She wanted to wait until he was on his own to see him, but she couldn't hold out that long. It would be worth the run-in with the mayor.

After their phone call the other night, she asked him for space. She needed the haze of the time they spent together to dissipate and the anxiety from his car accident to fade. He respected that, as he had all her boundaries. She didn't talk with her sisters or her parents about what she was doing. But she started sorting the things in her room and getting rid of anything that she wouldn't bring with her when she moved out.

She rang the buzzer on the gate and when it opened, proceeded to the front door. She clutched a small cardboard box.

The door opened before she got to the step, and Judy Caron stepped out.

"Ms. Blake, it's good to see you."

Alma held her tongue to keep herself from saying what she really wanted to say.

"Will is expecting me."

She opened the door wider for Alma to step in. "Yes, he's in the guest bedroom. It's down that hallway."

"Thank you." She went in the direction indicated.

"I know you two have a lot to talk about," Judy continued. "But I want you to know I came to an arrangement with your father. I'm dropping out of the race. Your father will likely be the next mayor."

Alma clenched her jaw. She didn't know what happened between Will and his mother in the days since he promised to ruin her for Alma. Will might have forgiven her, but that didn't mean Alma had to.

"You still hurt me with that article and tried to hurt me again."

"I know. And I'm truly sorry. I lost track of what is important. If I'm in your life more, then know I'm sorry and I don't blame you or him for being angry with me."

Alma didn't react. This could be real or arranged by her father. "I'm here to talk with Will."

She proceeded to the bedroom.

Taking several deep breaths, she knocked on the door, and Will told her to come in.

When she stepped inside, she saw him sitting on the bed,

with his booted leg propped up on a pillow, his hair rumpled, and wearing a T-shirt and boxers.

His eyes instantly lit up when he saw her. "Alma."

"Hi." She smiled.

"I thought I had more time. I wanted to shower. Nothing I'm wearing is clean." His hands moved around him, searching for something to cover himself.

"It's fine. I hoped to catch you unguarded."

"Sneaky." He pointed to the chair next to his bed. "Please, sit."

She did and placed the box on the nightstand. "I brought you a cupcake."

"Where's yours?"

"I ate it in the car." She'd been nervous. She didn't think he'd reject her, or tell her it was all a lie, but that didn't mean she looked forward to this conversation. She wanted it over and behind her.

She looked around the room, wondering if she'd learn anything about him.

"I've never lived here," he said, guessing at what she was doing. "I wanted to go to my apartment, the one by the club. It has an elevator. But my parents insisted I recover here."

"Your real apartment?"

"It's not far from here. But it's on the third floor, and I can't do stairs any time soon." He pointed to the boot on his leg. "You can have my keys and trash it."

"I don't want to trash your apartment or do any sort of revenge. I just want to know who you are."

He shook his head. "I know I lied and hid things from you, and I'm so sorry that I hurt you. But when it was us, that was me."

"What was fake then?" He could give her a list of everything real, but maybe it was easier to start with the lies. Maybe that list was shorter. She hoped it was shorter.

"The job, obviously. Any time it appeared like I wasn't into you. My mother was losing in the polls. She wanted to destroy your father. To do that, she went after you. You aren't as enmeshed in the family business as the rest of them. You do your own thing. She thought you were vulnerable."

"So, you went to see me in *Midsummer*."

"I did. You were so fucking amazing; I couldn't handle it. I watched after the show as you signed autographs, like a complete creep. I thought about asking you out. We had seventh-grade science together if you remember."

"Ocean currents." A class project they worked on together. "You spilled water all over me."

"I don't remember that." He smiled. Alma loved his smile.

"But you didn't ask me out."

"No. She threatened to cancel my funding. I didn't want Eros to fail right after it opened. I thought I could protect you and appease her."

"But then she sent in people with cocaine?" Alma had worked that detail out.

"Yes. I had nothing to do with that. I should have never gone along with her plan. I should have told you everything from the beginning. I'm so sorry, Alma. I know you have no reason to believe me, but everything was real. You are a goddess, and I don't deserve you. I'll spend the rest of my life making it up to you."

She inhaled sharply. He wasn't done with her. It was up to her to decide whether she was done with him.

"It was a very dumb plan," Alma said.

"I know." He reached for her hand and she held it tight. She'd missed his skin against hers.

The backs of his knuckles were covered in burn marks.

"What's this?" she asked.

"The airbag."

She hated that he was in pain.

"I tried to tell you on Saturday night." He didn't say it like he blamed her. More like he realized how weak he was when it came to her.

"I can be quite stubborn when I want something," she said.

He squeezed her hand. "I know my mother is stepping out of the race and endorsing your father. I told her it was up to you what you do about her schemes."

"I can't hurt you, so I won't go public. And I don't want my choices dragged through the media again." Through all her cleaning in the previous days, she came to that decision. Her father and Judy were coming to some sort of arrangement that she wanted nothing to do with. She'd no longer be mayor. Alma didn't want to drag Will down. "But I'm not ready to forgive her."

"You don't have to. I'm not sure I have."

"But you're here."

"I don't have much of a choice."

"What if I went with you to your apartment?" He'd said he'd spend his life making it up to her. They needed time and space to figure each other out and what brewed between them. This could be their chance.

"You don't have to," he said.

"What if it was me? What if I had the broken leg and the toxic parents?"

He broke eye contact as if he knew he was defeated. "I'd wait on you for as long as you needed."

"This is real then? We both want this?" she asked.

"Alma, I'm in love with you. I have been since you walked onto that stage. I know it's soon, but I'm in this if you'll give me the chance to prove myself."

She didn't hold back any longer. She wrapped her arms around his neck, hoping she wasn't hurting him, and rested her forehead on his. "I am falling in love with you, too. But

I'm scared. Because if this was a lie, I'll never be able to trust again."

"This is real, Alma. I swear to you." He leaned in to brush her lips gently with his. "I wanted to kiss you in my office and every moment after that. Every touch, every look, was real."

She pressed into him, opening her lips to allow him entry. This was real. This was the truth that could never be faked. For the first time with him, she didn't need any guards up. She let herself be *her* and rest in her feelings.

They broke apart, and she smiled.

"This means you can't smirk after I kiss you anymore," Will said.

"Don't worry; this isn't a performance."

"Good." He pulled her in, but she jerked away when he winced. "Sorry, we'll have to take this really slow."

"Slow can be good."

She eased herself out of his arms and walked to the other side of the bed. "Let's sit for a while." She cuddled up close to him as he grabbed the remote for the TV and unpaused the cooking show he had been watching.

He brushed her hair to one side of her neck and slowly stroked the skin on her arm. Together, they let the afternoon drift away, without any secrets between them.

Epilogue

Six weeks later, Will stood in the VIP lounge of Eros, one hand firmly in Alma's and the other resting on a pair of crutches.

He should sit and give his leg a rest; he had a long night ahead of him and was restricted by how long he was allowed to put weight on it. But sitting would mean he was farther from Alma. He wouldn't be able to reach her skin.

Her touch felt vital to his existence.

For the first time, no one in the club wore a mask.

It was Charles Blake's election night victory party. They waited for the official results, but no one worried. There were other candidates, but they lacked the name recognition of Charles Blake, especially once Judy Caron begrudgingly threw her support behind him.

The VIP room was reserved for family, high-level campaign staff, and the biggest donors. Which was why Alma was currently smiling and nodding while having the film audition process described to her by someone who had given a lot of money to her father. She was fulfilling her role as the future first daughter of Denver, being charming to anyone who wished to talk with her. Her sisters had the same task and were scattered in the club.

Alma hadn't landed any major roles since *Midsummer,* and her resilience was eroding. Charles allowed her to keep working part-time, but she worried he'd change his mind. She practically moved in with Will, claiming it was to help him get around and recover, but Will wanted it to be official. She said she didn't want to until she made enough money to pay half the rent. He understood that. She wanted to be independent and succeed on her own even if she chose to share her life with someone else. Tonight, he would propose a new step in their relationship—something to solve her living and job situations.

No secrets between them.

Will was sure they held up the no secrets part. Her trust in him was not a guarantee, and so every day, with his words, actions, and body, he showed her how much he loved her.

She hadn't said those words yet, but it was coming. He saw her feel it as strongly as he did.

He saw Alma's patience with the mansplaining fade.

"If you'll excuse us, I need to check on the bar, and I need Alma to accompany me." He almost added "for reasons," but caught himself. The excuse was flimsy enough.

They exchanged a few more pleasantries with the man before they headed to the bar. The club wasn't crowded. It was normally closed on Tuesday nights, so he was able to rent it out to the campaign. The dress code was gone and most of the crowd wore jeans and campaign T-shirts. Everyone's eyes were glued to their phones or the TV screens, waiting for updates. Will tracked the movement of his staff. Ben watched what normally was the dance floor but was instead where the press were set up. Max constantly moved from the bar to the VIP section. Many people were celebrating early.

When they got to the bar, Alma ordered them both a French 75. She'd been coming in to help him over the past few weeks and once the bartenders found out she hadn't drank much, they did cocktail tastings until she found one she liked. It turned out she had a predilection for gin.

He held his glass out in a toast. "What are we celebrating tonight?" He'd been careful around her feelings about her father and this election. It changed her life in ways she hadn't anticipated. It made her a target. She hadn't told Will everything she and her father had discussed in the days following their first weekend together, but she was determined to get away from his influence.

"To new beginnings," she said.

"To new beginnings." He savored the taste of gin and champagne on his tongue. "That's what I wanted to talk about with you tonight."

"Oh really?" She gave him a bit of side-eye, wondering where he was taking this. He didn't bring up his feelings unless necessary, wanting to give her space to process everything. But it was time.

"I've had some interesting meetings the last few days. Eros is doing exceptionally well, and people are noticing. An investor offered to partner with me for a club in New York."

"Really? That's amazing!" She launched herself at him, embracing him tightly. He rubbed his hands down her spine. He'd never tire of the feel of her.

"Yes, but this means I would have to move to New York." She adjusted to look at him. "I want you to come with me." It wasn't truly a want. It was an all-consuming need. If she didn't go with him, he'd stay in Denver. He needed her more than he needed any business opportunity.

"Wait. You just opened Eros. You can't leave."

"Eros is well managed. They don't need me overseeing the day-to-day."

"But what about our families?"

"Leaving them behind might be a bonus," Will said.

"It's not like either one of them needs our votes for another few years."

"Think of all the opportunities you'll have in New York."

"I don't have as much saved as I wanted."

He cut her off. "You have me. I'll always support you. But I have absolute faith in your ability to stand on your own."

She looked at him with her trusting eyes. Neither one of them wore masks anymore. All their flaws and fears were exposed for the other to see.

"I love you," she said. "Let's do this."

He kissed her, not caring that this was a public event and there were reporters around. Or that any one of their parents could see them.

"I love you, too," he said. He rested his forehead on hers.

"You're mine," she said. "Forever."

A Note on Elections

I can't write a book about elections without getting on my soapbox for a moment.

Love is always political.

Local and municipal elections are incredibly important. But they are frequently held apart from federal elections. Denver, for example, holds them in the spring. Depending on the city, these races might also be non-partisan meaning that no candidates will have a political party affiliation on the ballot. Many candidates will be from the same party, especially in cities that are a majority of one party.

Voting rights are under attack in many states, including Florida where I live. If you can vote, please do so and fight for the rights of people who are being marginalized. If your existence has not been legislated and your rights have not been decided by the Supreme Court, you have privilege and can fight for those that have less.

If you live in the United States, you can check your voter registration status at Iwillvote.com.

Acknowledgments

Publishing a book has been a dream of mine since I was a little kid. I know that I would not have made it this far without a lot of help.

My beta readers: Nicole McCurdy of Emerald Edits and Ally Reid. Ally, you were the first person to read this book. I thought it was good, and I'm so glad you agreed!

Sarah and Bess for hosting weekly write ins. This book wouldn't have happened without that accountability and the support of the rest of the Pubbers. #TeamTea

My sisters for tolerating every random text update and every slightly unhinged Instagram reel shared.

Kaely and Jessika, for being my friends since I was a teenager. Really this book wouldn't have happened without all those trips from Boulder to Denver in college and all the crying over the boys that didn't deserve us.

Samantha, I'm sorry for any election inaccuracies or misrepresentations.

My therapist – you helped me be a functional human again and gave me the brain space I needed to write this book.

And finally, my very sexy accountant, Wesley. You are the best husband I could ever hope for. You show me true love every day and prove that soulmates exists. I am sorry that I'll never understand what a Schedule C is on our tax returns. You see, you start talking about them, and you're so competent, and I just get distracted.

Okay, I'm not sorry about that.

Newsletter Sign Up

If you're not done with Will and Alma, you can sign up for my newsletter and get an exclusive bonus prequel and a bonus epilogue. In the bonus prequel, you'll get to see the moment when Will sees Alma onstage for the first time. You'll also be the first to hear about new book news, cover reveals, and more!

Sign up here: www.rebeccavarcher.com/newsletter

or scan the QR code:

About the Author

Rebecca V. Archer writes contemporary romance about characters who are afraid of their own emotions. She lives in Florida with her soulmate, drinks copious amounts of tea, and is always looking for a new cocktail or food recipe to try.

Check out her website for updates.

www.rebeccavarcher.com